Harvest Wishes

a STARLIGHT INN novel

Jessica Anne Renwick

Published by Starfell Press

Starlight Inn Book One
Harvest Wishes

ISBN (paperback) 978-1-989854-06-8
ISBN (eBook) 978-1-989854-05-1

Cover design by Ana Grigoriu-Voicu, www.books-design.com
Edited by Talena Winters, www.talenawinters.com
Formatting by Red Umbrella Graphic Designs and Formatting
Proofread by Erin Dyrland
Author Photo © Bonny-Lynn Marchment. Used by permission.

MORE BY JESSICA ANNE RENWICK

THE STARLIGHT INN

Harvest Wishes
Novel Dreams
Holiday Hopes

Pumpkin Promises

Thank you all so much to all of my loved ones who supported me through the creation of my own new chapter of life. I wouldn't be where I am today without you.

CHAPTER ONE

"What does a handsome guy like you see in a girl like me?" Madison Talbot gave Monty, a golden retriever-mix, a pat on his head. He licked her hand, gazing up at her with wide brown eyes and let out a whine.

"Aw, don't look at me like that. I promise I'll be back Thursday. You can manage to wait two days, right?" She scratched his ears, then let herself out of his kennel and closed the latch. A pen swung from a string tied to the clipboard attached to the wire door. She grabbed it and scribbled *walk from 1:30 to 2:00* on Monty's sheet and signed her initials beside it.

The dog gave her a baleful look through the wire, then plodded to his bed in the corner.

Poor old guy, I hope he finds a home soon. Madison gave him one last look, then made her way past the other enclosures—some with dogs pressed up against the gates, barking as she passed, and others snuggled into their beds like Monty—and into the front lobby of Pawsitive Match pet rescue.

Photos of proud dogs with their smiling new families were plastered on the bright blue walls. Like she did every day she volunteered here, she found the photo of a brindle Great Dane-mix with droopy jowls. Mack, whom she adopted from this rescue two years ago, gazed at the camera. In the photo, Madison had her arm around his bulky shoulders and a huge grin on her face. She chuckled at the thought of the dog at her parents' house right now, probably forcing her Mom's toy poodle, Dolly, to cuddle with him on his giant bed in the living room. As she smiled, a stray lock of hair fell into her face. She pulled the scrunchy from her ponytail, letting her chocolate-brown waves fall over her shoulders, and slipped it around her wrist.

Her gaze shifted to the poster next to the pictures. A cute drawing of pawprints in the shape of a heart stood out next to the title—*Donations Needed*!

Beneath it was a list of supplies and the contact information for the shelter. She frowned, thinking of her empty bank account. *I wish I could do more to help.*

"Done for the day, Madison?" The rescue's administrator, Danica, asked from her seat behind the front desk. Her tight black curls were pulled back into a frizzy bun, and brown paw prints stained her blue scrubs.

Madison turned and approached the counter to sign out. "Yep. Dexter was full of himself today. He tried to take off after a squirrel, but I managed to hang on." She paused, thinking of the yellow-coated dog she had just put away. "Monty seemed off again, though. Sluggish and not really into the walking thing. I don't know how to help him. I hope he gets adopted soon."

Danica gave her a sad smile. "I wish we could find somebody to foster him. I think he'd do a lot better in a home than here in all that chaos." She gestured toward the kennel area, where another volunteer led a shepherd-looking dog from the bathing station to its kennel, causing an eruption of barks and yips from the others.

"I would totally take him if I could." Madison scrawled her signature on the sign-out form and placed the pen on top of it. "But you know, I'm not exactly set up for that." Her cheeks warmed at the mention of her living situation. *Back home with Mom and Dad. At twenty-eight years old, after an epically failed marriage. No job, no money, no life.* She blew at a loose tress of her hair. *Could be worse, right? Mack and I could be on the street.*

"Not yet." Danica leaned back in her chair and shot Madison a kind smile. "But you'll be back on your feet before you know it. I'm sure Mack would love a buddy to hang with all day."

Or maybe he'd prefer a stable owner who doesn't truck him across the province and force him from house-to-house?

She swallowed the lump in her throat, thinking of Mack's drooly smile and the way he bounded to the door to greet her every time she came home. "He has Mom's dog, Dolly, for now. But once I'm on my own, maybe he'll need a buddy."

"Everybody needs a buddy," Danica agreed, then got to her feet and leaned her elbows on the counter.

"You know, I'm having drinks with some friends tonight at Last Call," she said. "You're welcome to join us. I have a friend you might like to meet."

"No thanks," Madison replied, immediately regretting her curt tone. She softened her gaze. "I mean, I'm not really ready for socializing yet. At least, not that way. You know?"

"Of course." Danica gave her a sympathetic look. "But when you're up for it, my friend is *really* nice. He's a teacher at the elementary school and great with kids. Gentle. He'd never—" she hesitated, glancing at Madison from the corner of her eye—"you know. He's not an angry guy."

Madison fought the urge to roll her eyes. Everybody in town had a *really nice* friend to introduce her to. That's the problem with growing up in a small town like Cedar Lake in the Fraser Valley of British Columbia, everybody knows you and everybody knows your business.

I've only been back for three weeks and the whole town's talking. But she'd known that would happen when she left her six-year marriage and moved home from Vancouver. The people here just couldn't help it.

Madison Talbot, daughter of the beloved Dr. Bill Talbot and his wife, Paula, the town's event-planner. Back at home. Life in tatters. Reeling from an abusive marriage! She was surprised she hadn't yet been the talk of the community's gossipy Facebook group, *Cedar Lake Local Updates.*

Maybe I have. I better check that. She cringed. *On second thought, maybe it's better not to know.*

"Anyways," Danica continued, "when you're ready, let me know. We could go out as a group, so it's not as awkward."

"Yeah. Cool. Maybe someday." Madison shifted uneasily and glanced at the door. "I better get going. I'm supposed to meet Sophie at the Starlight Inn in a few minutes. You know, she's the main chef there now. On a tight schedule for the dinner rush."

"Lucky! That place is gorgeous." Danica gave her a little wave. "See you Thursday."

"See you then." Madison rapped her fingers on the counter, then strode to the door. She couldn't get out of there fast enough. Just as she reached the entrance, the door swung open and a man with familiar-looking dark brows and a surly expression marched through, bumping into her.

Her chest seized and panic shot to her head. She stepped back, holding her leather handbag in front of her like a shield.

The man flicked his gaze to hers. His eyes were brown, not the piercing green she'd been expecting. Her heartbeat slowed, and she lowered her purse. She'd never seen this man before. *He's not Jamie. Geez, Madison Calm down. You're losing it.*

"Uh, hey. Sorry about that." He gave her a peculiar look, then made his way to the front desk.

"Madison?" Danica leaned around him. "You okay?"

"I'm fine." Madison stammered, her neck hot. "See you Thursday." Taking a deep breath, she pushed outside and let the cool fall air fill her lungs. The fog in her mind lifted, and the moment the October sunshine hit her skin, her tension melted away.

Her old, blue Nissan car sat in front of a red-leafed maple tree at the other end of the parking lot. Rusted and saggy, it looked sad next to the shiny, new Toyota sedan parked next to it. But it was her own set of wheels, and all she could afford after leaving everything behind, including her bookkeeping job in the city.

She hadn't needed a vehicle in Vancouver, and the newfound freedom of jumping in and taking off at a moment's notice thrilled her. No planning ahead or rushing to a bus stop. *Or relying on somebody who wants to keep me home.* She sauntered toward it, trying to calm her mind with every step.

She pulled the driver's door open and collapsed inside. "What is wrong with me? As if Jamie would ever come to Cedar Lake." With trembling hands, she sifted through the empty candy wrappers in her cup holder and pulled out a Ziploc bag filled with Fuzzy Peach candies. She opened it and popped one in her mouth, letting the fizzy tang overwhelm her senses.

I have a restraining order against him. He's too concerned with his image to break that, she reminded herself. *Besides, he's not ambitious enough to drive two hours to start a fight. And he's scared of Dad and Marshal.* The man hadn't even contested her court-ordered divorce. They had lived in a rental, and with no big assets to split, Madison had been happy to walk away with not much more than her dog and the clothes on her back. Given the charges against her ex-husband, she hadn't had to adhere to a separation period.

The divorce had been granted, the paperwork signed and sealed, in less than two weeks.

Just as I wanted. She grabbed another candy from the bag, zipped it closed, and tossed it on the passenger seat.

She pulled her phone from her purse and glanced at the time. *2:10. Twenty minutes to get out to the Starlight Inn for a quick coffee with Sophie before the dinner rush.* Sophie Walsh, her best friend since junior high and now girlfriend to her twin brother, Marshal, was the head chef at the quaint inn just outside of town. They'd drifted apart after she moved to Vancouver six years ago to be with Jamie. Now that she was back, Madison vowed to make it up to Sophie. To rekindle their friendship and never let it slip away again.

She glanced in the rear-view mirror at the box in her back seat. *The best way to Sophie's heart? Food, of course.* Inside that box sat a giant cherry cheesecake from Josie's Diner. Sure, Sophie could easily whip up something a lot better, but this cake was special. As teens, the girls would hang out at Josie's and share one of the huge slices of cheesecake every time something big happened in their lives.

Be it graduation, Sophie passing her culinary classes with flying colours, even Madison and Jamie's engagement—eating cake at Josie's had been one of their rituals.

Her phone buzzed in her hand, and she glanced down to see Sophie's name light up the screen. She swiped it open.

Are we still on for 2:30? Just to warn you— Dylan just called and he's on his way with a delivery from Marshal. I understand if you want to back out. We can do coffee tomorrow instead.

Madison's heart twinged. Dylan Stewart, her ex-boyfriend from high school. The guy who took off for Vancouver with a scholarship to U.B.C. after graduation, canceling their trip to backpack around Europe that fall. A trip they'd had planned for two years. Effectively, ending their relationship. In other words, the second-last person she wanted to see right now, aside from Jamie.

I can't believe Marshal had him do the delivery today. He knew I was going over there. Guilt pricked her side. Marshal owned the market garden that delivered produce to the inn.

He'd been run off his feet this week with harvesting the fall produce and making deliveries all over the valley. If Madison hadn't been volunteering at Pawsitive Match today, she probably would have made the delivery herself.

She bit the side of her cheek. *I guess I didn't leave Marshal much choice.*

But she couldn't let Dylan ruin her coffee date with Sophie. This was important. And besides, she and Dylan had ended things ten years ago. She couldn't hold a grudge forever. *Water under the bridge, right?*

She sent Sophie a quick reply: *No worries. I'll be there in a few minutes. With a surprise!*

Besides, how long would it take him to drop off a few boxes of vegetables? She tossed her phone into the car's console, then grabbed the bag of candy. She popped another Fuzzy Peach into her mouth and backed her car from its parking spot.

He'll probably be gone before I even get there.

Her heart lifted. She flipped on the car's radio and turned onto the quiet street, allowing herself to enjoy the moment of normalcy in her turbulent life.

CHAPTER TWO

"There you go, Mom. That should do it." Dylan Stewart stood in his mother's kitchen, screwdriver in one hand and the other on the handle to her screen door. He swung it closed, then gave it a good jiggle to make sure it had latched. "I tightened the hinges, so it should hang straight now. At least until the next time you get angry and ninja-kick it open," he teased.

"Please." His mom, Cathy, crossed her arms and leaned her hip on the kitchen table. "You know I couldn't do that even if I wanted to."

Dylan glanced at his mother, whose head barely reached his shoulder. "I don't know, Justine told me you've been working out. By the look of this door a few minutes ago, I'd say it's paying off."

"Ha!" She shook her head, but her wavy grey-streaked brown hair—the only feature Dylan had inherited from her—barely moved. "I'm not sure if yoga is going to give me muscles like that. But it's helping with my headspace, if anything. Christine was right," she said, referring to her best friend. "It's good for the soul."

Dylan closed his dad's rusty toolbox and placed it in its usual spot under the sink. *Good for the soul*, he mused. She did seem happier lately. Even alone in this old house, surrounded by memories of his dad and Ryan. He glanced at the calendar that hung beside the door, a firetruck-red 1948 Ford F1 on the faded paper.

"Why don't you get rid of that old thing?" He gestured toward it. "Put up something you'd like; with roses or kittens or something. Or those weird babies sitting in flower pots. And the correct year would help."

"You know I like keeping his things out. It makes it feel like he's still around." Cathy gave him a sad smile.

He flicked his gaze to the old family photo on the shelf above the oak table against the wall—their perfect, smiling family. Twelve years ago, when Dylan was in grade eleven. Before the accident.

Even then, he had stood tall and lanky like his father, John. He swallowed and flicked his gaze to his mom. *Ryan looked more like her, with those blue eyes, freckled skin that burnt within five minutes in the sun, and that wide smile. It probably kills her to look at me—the spitting image of Dad.*

He shook his head. "Isn't it better to just put a few of his mementos away and clean out this place? Make it your own. Every time I walk in here, it's like a blast from the past. A hard past."

"I like it that way. It reminds me of the good times, before the car accident. I don't feel as lonely."

Guilt tugged at Dylan's heart. He hated that she wallowed in this house alone.

"Alright. I won't push it." He paused, trying to think of something to lighten the mood. "Have you been over to see Natalie lately?" He asked, referring to his five-year-old niece—Ryan's daughter and the biggest piece of his mother's heart. Of both their hearts, really. "Her birthday's coming up, and Justine told me she'd like us to come over."

Cathy's face lit up. "I was just there on the weekend to see her practice for her dance recital.

She said she has a surprise for you."

Dylan crossed his arms and raised a brow. "Should I be worried? Last time she had a surprise for me, it involved water balloons and a Super Soaker."

Cathy let out a giggle, holding her side. "No, nothing like that. I won't spoil it for you, but it's perfectly harmless. I promise."

Dylan pressed his lips together, teasing her. "You said that about the water balloons, too."

The lines around her eyes crinkled with her laugh. "Oh Dylan, she's going to miss you when you're gone. I am too."

He cringed. "I know, Mom. I'm sorry. I don't have much choice. If I had it my way, I'd stay. But my boss—"

"It's okay, hon." His mom shot him a sympathetic look. "I know."

He swallowed the lump in his throat. It'd been over two years since he left Vancouver to be with his Mom and Justine—his brother's widow—after the accident. He worked in IT for a tech corporation, and his boss had graciously allowed him to work from home most of the time.

After renting an apartment in Cedar Lake a few blocks from his childhood home, he'd set up his workspace there and only went to the city once a week for meetings. It had been working perfectly, but now the company was growing and his boss's patience was waning. He wanted Dylan back at the office daily, and he wanted it soon. In the new year, Dylan was moving back to Vancouver—whether he liked it or not.

"I'll keep working on Jason," Dylan said, referring to his boss. "Honestly, there's no reason for me to move back. These last two years have proved that."

"You have to do what's best for you." Cathy moved to his side and patted his forearm. "I know there's not much work here in Cedar Lake with computer stuff. At least we'll have Christmas together."

His chest tightened. *And then what? I leave Justine struggling to keep up with Natalie and her job at the hospital, and you sitting alone in this house talking to Dad and Ryan as if they're still around?* He scrubbed his face with his palm. *At least when I'm here, I can pull her back to reality.*

"Right. Christmas." He rubbed his jaw. "We'll have to come up with something big for Natalie."

"Definitely," Cathy agreed. She glanced at the ornamental clock, set into the box of a porcelain red pick-up truck, on the shelf next to their family photo and clucked her tongue. "It's after two. Don't you have to get those vegetable boxes to the Starlight Inn for Marshal?"

"That I do." Dylan pulled his mom in for a hug then made his way to the door, fighting the urge to remove the calendar from the wall beside it. "Think about replacing the calendar, okay? Christine probably thinks you're going nuts every time she comes over and sees it."

Cathy grinned and shook her head. "No, she doesn't. She thinks it is a perfectly normal way to stay connected with our loved ones. Sometimes I feel them here, and she agrees."

"Of course she does." Dylan shook his head. Christine Walsh, his mom's best friend, was the owner of Steeped in Books, the book and tea shop downtown. She was also his friend Sophie's mom, and had recently gotten into a lot of weird, new-agey stuff. She had even brought meditation necklaces and strange herbal concoctions into her store.

All a bunch of hocus pocus baloney. He glanced at his mom over his shoulder. "Well, if you see Dad popping out of the basement, say hi."

"He's usually sitting at his desk in the living room, where he used to do his puzzles."

Dylan's neck stiffened, and he hesitated with his hand on the doorknob, unsure if she was kidding or not. He gave her a sideways glance, and she smirked. *Please tell me she's joking.* "You okay?"

She picked up the copper kettle from the stove and began to fill it from the tap above the old farmhouse sink. "Perfectly fine. Now get going, you're going to be late. Don't want to catch Sophie during the supper rush."

"Right. You sure you're okay?" Dylan looked at her again, studying the lines on her face. Her gaze met his, her blue eyes bright with mischief. *She looks healthy...*

"I'm fine. Go!"

"Alright, alright." He waved goodbye and pushed through the door, satisfied with the click of the latch behind him, then made his way to his black Ford Explorer. He hopped inside and glanced in his rear-view mirror at the boxes of produce in the back.

A quick stop at the Starlight Inn, then home for a four o'clock meeting and an evening of work. That was one of the perks of working from home, his company allowed him to make his own hours outside of video meetings. His stomach knotted at the thought of losing this—his daily life in his sleepy hometown, his Mom, and Natalie. If the tragedies his family had gone through taught him anything, it was that life was short and his loved ones were most important.

More important than some job I don't even like for some big corporation. He gazed at the wicker bench on his mom's front porch, remembering the way his parents used to sit out there drinking tea on summer evenings. His stomach clenched at the unfairness of it all.

His dad had been diagnosed with colon cancer when Dylan was in grade twelve. It had been a driving factor in his flight to Vancouver, where he buried his feelings in school and partying with his friends. When his dad's cancer had gone into remission a few years later, it had seemed like the world had righted. Like everything was back in place.

And to have it all ripped away by some drunk driver. The man who'd beat cancer. The big brother who could defeat anything. Dylan closed his eyes. *I can't leave Mom here alone.*

He grabbed his phone from the console and pulled up Sophie's name and hit call.

It rang twice, and then, "Hello?"

"Hey, Sophie. It's Dylan. I'm on my way with Marshal's delivery. He had to run like two dozen pumpkins to Jacksons' farm for their carving contest," he said. "Sorry I'm a bit behind, had to stop at my mom's first."

He was met with silence.

"Sophie, you there?"

Sophie let out a breath. "I'm here. Marshal told me this morning you'd be coming." She paused. "Um. Just drive around back when you get here. There might be—well, just to warn you, Madison might be here. She's coming for coffee. I should have had Marshal tell you."

Dylan's heart lurched. "Madison Talbot?"

"The one and only."

Okay. I can handle this. We broke up ten years ago. No biggie, right? He bit back a groan. "Yeah, no problem. I won't bother you ladies.

I'll just unload these boxes and get out of your hair."

"Perfect," Sophie replied, her tone cautious. "See you soon."

"See ya."

He hung up and shoved his phone in his jacket pocket, the image of Madison's deep brown eyes boring into his mind. Part of him was sure she hated him for taking off to college and canceling their Europe trip. But he'd had no choice, he would have lost his scholarship if he put off school. However, he could have handled it better, instead of putting off the decision until the last minute. And then hiding it from her until it was made.

After their break-up, she'd married that weasel, Jamie. Who they all saw coming from a mile away. *But what could I have done? It's not like she would have listened to me.* And now she was back, tending a broken heart. Probably despising him even more than ever.

He closed his eyes, guilt churning inside him. *I'll just drop off the vegetables and go. If I'm quick, I might even get out of there before she arrives.*

He threw the Explorer into reverse and cranked the radio, ignoring the ache in his chest.

CHAPTER THREE

Madison hummed along with the radio, enjoying the view of the countryside. She pulled up to a white sign with the words the Starlight Inn scrawled across it in gold letters and turned into the approach next to it. A rail fence lined the gravel drive on either side of her, and horses grazed in the pastures against a backdrop of red and orange from the changing leaves. A Victorian-style inn with a wide front porch sat at the end of the driveway. Twinkle lights hung from the porch roof, and bushes filled with merlot-coloured leaves skirted the front.

Sophie is so lucky to work here. What I would give to land a job at this place. Madison pulled her car around to the back entrance of the kitchen, her stomach tight.

Even though it had been several weeks since she left Vancouver, she'd only just begun her job hunt in Cedar Lake. She'd wanted to get her head on straight first, and with her experience in office administration and accounting, she'd thought it would be easy to find a job here. But Cedar Lake was small, and there wasn't much opportunity.

She parked next to a black Ford Explorer on the parking pad behind the inn, then hopped out of her car and grabbed the cake box from the back seat. Carefully balancing it in two hands, she made her way up the stairs, admiring the cedar stable that sat at the end of a twisty path through the trees. Madison paused in front of the door, watching a young man grooming a dappled grey horse tied to the hitching post in the corral attached to the barn. *Cozy inn, romantic trails, horses—this place has it all.*

She shifted the cake box to her side and rapped on the door with her free hand. The sound of footsteps met her ears. Assuming they belonged to Sophie, she twisted the handle, then pushed on the door with her hip. Suddenly, it swung open, and Madison's stomach turned as she began to fall. *No, no, no!*

The cake box slipped from her side to the floor, and somebody with strong arms caught her around the waist.

"Whoa! You okay?"

The voice tugged at her memory—deep and velvety smooth.

"The cake!" She twisted to get her feet under her, leaning into the man who caught her. She gripped his firm forearms beneath a layer of soft flannel and righted herself. Her hair had fallen into her face and she tossed it behind her shoulders, then looked up at the man towering over her—gazing right into a pair of all-too-familiar brown eyes. Combined with that dimple in his chin and the dark hair that curled at the edges—

Dylan Stewart!

Madison stepped backward, pushing him away. "Dylan. Uh… hey."

He rubbed the back of his neck and gave her the same sheepish smile he'd had for her when they were teenagers. The first time he asked her to the movies. When he'd accidentally flipped their kayak on their school trip in grade eleven. That night they'd camped beneath the stars in Glacier Park…

"Madison! Hey. I heard you were back in town." He paused, sweeping her with his gaze. "You okay?"

Her heart raked against her chest. Without thinking, she looked him up and down. *No. No. No. Why does he look like that?* The last time she'd seen him was over five years ago at a mutual friend's wedding, and he'd been thin as a rail in his baggy suit. *Now*—she swallowed and ran her hand through her tangled locks. "I'm fine. Thanks."

He shrugged, then bent down to pick up the dented cake box. "I'm not sure if your cake is okay—sorry about that. I didn't mean, well, you know. I just meant to open the door."

"It's fine. Totally fine. No worries." Madison took the cake from him with trembling hands, her neck hot. Her heart sank at the sight of the caved-in corner of the box. *Hopefully it's okay.*

Dylan shoved his hands in his pockets and rocked back on his heels, gazing at her with humour in his eyes. "Good to bump into you again. Literally. It's been a while."

"Yeah. I'll say. Great to see you." Madison hugged the box to her chest, her cheeks flaming.

The perfect way to show my ex-boyfriend how great I'm doing—literally fall on him and stare at him like a fish. Good job, Madison. Keep up the fantastic image. Why don't you tell him all about living in your parents' basement and your unemployment too?

She glanced up at him, and he raised his brows with that amused look she remembered so well. *There was never a serious bone in his body.* At least, not until his dad had been diagnosed with cancer when they were in grade twelve. Her chest hitched at the memory, and the way he'd pulled away from her that year. It was as if he'd built a stone fortress around his heart—and not even she had been allowed in. She had heard his dad went into remission a few years later, and had been happy about the news. But by then, the rift between her and Dylan was so wide that she hadn't felt comfortable enough to call him.

Besides, he left me. Practically ghosted. Cancelled our Europe trip last minute and disappeared to Vancouver. Her spine stiffened, and she cleared her throat. "I better get this cake—or what's left of it—inside to Sophie."

His face fell, and he gave her a curt nod. "Right."

"Madison!" As if on cue, Sophie appeared in the doorway, her face flush and her copper hair sticking out in flyaway strands from her hairnet. "You're here. I'm sorry, I was just going over tonight's menu with one of the guests who has a shellfish allergy." She looked at Dylan and took a sharp inhale. "Dylan. You're still here."

"I was just on my way out when Madison knocked on the door."

Madison pressed her lips together. *Fell through the door is more like it.*

He glanced at his watch, his brow furrowed. "I should hit the road. I have a meeting at four."

"Sounds good." Sophie waved him off. "Thanks for bringing the veggies over."

"You bet. See you Friday night at Marshal's?"

Sophie tugged at her hair net, looking at Madison from the corner of her eye. "Ah—yep. Seven o'clock. We're having a fire outside, so dress warm."

A fire at Marshal's? Madison frowned. Her brother hadn't invited her.

"Sounds good," Dylan said with that easy grin. He flicked his gaze to Madison. "Are you going to come?"

"Uh…" Madison shifted uneasily, wishing the floor would just open up and eat her. She looked at Sophie. "Maybe?"

"Alright. Maybe see you then." He tipped his head to them, then strode out the door and closed it behind him.

Madison let out a breath, watching him retreat through the door's window.

Sophie gave Madison an earnest look. "I'm so sorry! I was trying to rush him out of here, but I got distracted."

"It's okay," Madison interjected. "It was just Dylan, not an ax murderer. At least, I doubt he's taken up serial killing in the last ten years. It's not really a hobby one gets into."

"The last thing I want is to make you uncomfortable," Sophie replied. "Marshal said you two still haven't spoken since—you know."

"Since he ditched out on our Europe trip and moved to Vancouver?" Madison replied dryly. "Honestly, Sophie. It's not a big deal. It was ten years ago. In case you forgot, I married and divorced somebody else since then. I'm not exactly pining for him anymore."

He did look good in those jeans though. When did he get so—strong? And the way he smiled…

She shook her head. *Stop it. Thinking about Dylan Stewart, of all people, is the absolute last thing I need right now.*

"I didn't say you were pining for him," Sophie replied, giving her a sly look. "But if you are, I wouldn't blame you. I mean—"

"I'm not." Madison lifted her chin and shifted the dented cake box. "But I am curious about this fire at Marshal's on Friday. Why wasn't I invited?"

"He just planned it yesterday. I'm sure Marshal didn't mean anything, he just hasn't had time to call you yet."

Well he had time to phone Dylan, apparently.

"Besides," Sophie squeezed her shoulder, "I'm inviting you now. It'll be a good chance for you to catch up with old friends."

Oh, joy. More people to explain my situation to. Madison bit the side of her cheek. "How many people are coming?"

"Just a few. You know Marshal, he's not exactly one to host a huge party. Please come?" Sophie said. "I promise, I won't let anybody pressure you into talking about you-know-who."

"Alright," Madison replied. "I'll come. Now, look at this broken gift I brought you."

Sophie's gaze fell on the box in Madison's hands. "Is that what I think it is?"

"If you're thinking it's cheesecake from Josie's Diner, then yes."

"Oh my goodness." Sophie let out a squeal and flung her arms around Madison's shoulders. "The best surprise!"

"You better take it before it gets squished even more." Madison laughed, holding the box to the side as she squirmed from her friend's arms.

"Come on! I've got about twenty minutes for coffee and a snack in the dining room. Tad just stepped out for a walk," she said, referring to her assistant. "It's just us. Follow me." Sophie led the way into the warm kitchen, a skip in her step.

The smell of freshly baked bread, warm coffee, and earthy spices wafted over Madison as she entered the room. Sophie set the cake on the kitchen island and lifted the lid.

"It's a bit squished and messy," she said. "But it'll taste perfect, all the same."

She showed Madison where the mugs were and they poured themselves coffees. After cutting two lop-sided pieces and placing them on plates, she gestured for Madison to follow her through the French doors to the dining area.

Sophie weaved through the mostly empty tables. Other than an older couple playing crib in the corner, the lunch guests had cleared out. She chose a table for two next to the crackling fireplace.

Once they were both settled, Sophie took a sip of her coffee. "So? How's everything going?"

"With what? The lawyers? The job hunt? The living with overbearing parents?" Madison sighed and flipped her hair behind her shoulder. *Stumbling like an idiot into the arms of my hot ex-boyfriend?*

"That's not what I meant." Sophie leaned her head toward her. "You shouldn't be so harsh with yourself. I'm really proud of you. Marshal is too."

Madison's throat thickened and she flicked her gaze to the fireplace. "Come on."

"I mean it," Sophie said firmly. "You're like a phoenix, rising from the ashes. Just you wait. You're moving in the right direction."

Madison swallowed, then took a swig of her coffee. She glanced at Sophie's earnest expression, her soft green eyes. "Look, leaving Jamie is the best thing I've ever done, and I do see a better future for myself. I just can't help but wonder, where would I be if I hadn't married him?" A question she'd been asking herself every day for the last few months. "There were so many warning signs."

"You can't think like that," Sophie replied. "It's so hard to get out, and you did it. You should be proud—"

"Proud of what?" Madison cut in. "Of falling for all his lies and letting him manipulate me for seven years?" *For staying even after he cheated on me? After he called me every name in the book?* A lump formed in her throat. *After the first time he got physically violent?* She couldn't even bring herself to form the words.

Sophie's face crumpled, and she reached across the table and squeezed Madison's arm. "I'm sorry, Madi. I didn't mean—"

The clattering of heels against the hardwood floor met Madison's ears, and she twisted in her chair. A woman wearing a plum-coloured pantsuit that perfectly complemented the dusky tones of her skin strode toward them, her gaze locked in Sophie's direction. Her ebony curls were pinned up behind her head and she held a clipboard tightly to her chest.

She gestured to an empty chair from the table beside them. "Sophie. Mind if I have a seat? This will be quick."

Sophie cast Madison a rueful glance and pushed her plate to the side. "Hey, Katie. Sure. This is my good friend, Madison. Marshal's sister. Madison, this is Katie. My boss and owner of the Starlight Inn."

"Nice to meet you, Madison." Katie pulled up a chair and plopped down into it. She ran a hand over her forehead and sighed. "We have an issue regarding the harvest festival."

"The harvest festival?" Sophie echoed. "It's only two weeks away."

"Yes." Katie nodded. "I know. Fiona with Fiona's Farm Pets pulled out. Apparently, her trailer broke down, and it won't be fixed in time. So, we have no petting zoo or pony rides. No main attraction for the kids."

"Oh no." Sophie's face fell. "So what do we have left?"

"Just the hayrides and the pumpkin patch." Katie shrugged with defeat. "Hot chocolate. That's about it."

"Well, the hayrides are fun. And maybe Dane and Evan could offer pony rides on some of the quieter horses," Sophie suggested.

Katie pressed her lips together. "Do you think that's enough? I don't want to disappoint our guests who booked this weekend specifically for the fall atmosphere and fun. And I had hoped to attract some attention from town to drum up business for our holiday sleigh rides."

"We could do some kind of charity fundraiser? Maybe a mitten tree for the homeless shelter?"

Katie pursed her lips. "That's nice, but not really something fun for families."

A fundraiser... Madison thought back to the donation poster at Pawsitive Match and to Monty's sad gaze through the kennel door. She leaned forward in her chair. "I have an idea. What about a donation drive for the dog shelter? I volunteer there, and they're always in need of supplies. They could even bring a few of the dogs here for meet-and-greets."

Katie looked at Madison. "What could we offer to drive donations and get people out here? The meet-and-greet sounds nice, but we need more of an activity."

"What about family photos at the pumpkin patch?"

Madison asked, excitement rising in her chest. "People love fall family portraits. And they could even bring their dogs for cute pet photos."

"That could totally work!" Sophie said. "My friend Isla is a photographer, and she's a huge dog lover. I could ask if she'd do the photos for a day rate. Anything we make above that could be donated to the shelter?"

Madison nodded in agreement. "And we could ask people to bring dog food and toys to donate in exchange for a pumpkin or something."

"I bet Marshal would donate some pumpkins for that." Sophie grinned and took a drink of her coffee. "And I could bake some pumpkin muffins or homemade dog treats to donate. What do you think, Katie?"

Katie leaned back in her chair, balancing the clipboard on her crossed knee. "I think that could work. People do love to support the shelter. Madison, if you have time, I could use some help with these last-minute changes. With your ties to Pawsitive Match—"

"I can totally help!" Madison gave her an eager grin. "Leave the Pawsitive Match stuff to me. I'm volunteering there Thursday, but I'll call them tonight to give them a heads up."

Katie nodded and scribbled some notes on her clipboard, then handed Madison her phone. "Add your number, and let me know how the talk with the shelter goes. Thank you so much for offering to do this. I think it could be a hit with the locals."

Madison added her number to Katie's phone and handed it back to her, then Katie got to her feet and gave them a nod. "We'll be in touch. Have a nice afternoon, ladies."

"Thanks, Katie." Sophie waved her off, then glanced at her watch. She looked at Madison. "I better get back to work. We'll talk about this more later. Friday night at Marshal's fire?"

"Sure," Madison agreed. Her stomach tightened as her thoughts shifted to Friday.

It will be fine. I need to get used to seeing people again, even Dylan. Besides, now I have something to talk about other than my failed marriage. She picked up her dishes and followed Sophie to the kitchen, her mind reeling with thoughts of hayrides, pumpkins, and her furry friends.

Chapter Four

"Hey, kiddo." Dylan ruffled his niece's dark frizzy hair, then opened the side door of his Explorer for her to climb in. Every Wednesday he picked up Natalie after school. Her mom, Justine, had a nursing shift that ended at two-thirty on Wednesdays—too close to kindergarten pickup for her to make it on time. That's where the world's best uncle stepped in, according to Natalie. And despite being her only uncle, Dylan was more than happy to be bestowed with that title.

"Hey!" Natalie grinned at him, a gap where one of her front teeth should be. "Watch the hair." She pushed her bangs from her face, straightened her polka-dot jacket, then climbed inside and into her car seat.

"Sorry, Sprout." Dylan watched as she buckled her straps, then checked them to make sure they were done up correctly.

"I'm too big to be called Sprout," Natalie replied. "Mom said when I'm six, I'll get to move up to a big-girl seat. So, like," she counted on her fingers, "in a week?"

"A little over a week," he said. "What should I call you then? Sapling?"

"What's a sapling?"

Dylan chuckled and stepped back. "A partially grown tree. A step above a sprout."

He closed the door, then rounded the vehicle to hop in the driver's seat. Two years ago, he would have never guessed he'd be doing school runs at this point in his life. He'd been living the singles scene in Vancouver, his only worries involving work and playing video games with his friends. Maybe the odd date. But since Madison, he hadn't had a relationship last for more than a few months. And never anything serious.

He glanced in the rear-view mirror at Natalie, who gave him a toothy smile. If he was the spitting image of his dad, then Natalie was the girl-version of Ryan.

Sure, her complexion was more olive than pale like his brother's had been, but that wide smile and those earthy brown eyes were all Ryan. And that silly personality—they had always been two peas in a pod. *If only she'd had more time with him.*

He put the car in drive and pulled out of the school parking lot and onto the street.

"How was school?"

"Awesome! We made bat puppets on popsicle sticks! We're doing a Halloween play with them."

"That sounds pretty cool," Dylan replied.

His phone vibrated in its dashboard holder. Keeping his eyes on the road, he hit the answer button and waited for the Bluetooth to click on. "Hello?"

"Hey, it's Marshal," Marshal Talbot, Dylan's best friend for over twenty years, said over the speakers.

"Hi Marshal!" Natalie shouted from the back.

"You got me and Natalie here," Dylan replied. "Just running her home from school." He stuck his tongue out at her in the mirror, and she covered her mouth to stifle a giggle.

"Hey, Natalie. How was school?" Marshal asked.

"Good. We made puppets today." She pulled her mitts from her hands and tossed them in the seat next to her.

"Puppets? Sounds fun," Marshal said. "Dylan, I have a favour to ask."

"Is it another hare-brained scheme to search every store in Cedar Lake for pumpkins or radishes or something like that?" Dylan asked, a smile tugging at his lips.

Marshal's market garden supplied produce to the Starlight Inn and many other small businesses in town. Only a few short weeks ago, he had called Dylan in a panic over a bunch of sugar pumpkins he'd promised to Sophie that had been destroyed by frost. After hours of hitting every grocery store in Cedar Lake and a pumpkin patch in another community, they'd managed to scrounge up more than what she needed.

"No," Marshal replied dryly. "But it is for the inn. And weirdly, pumpkins. You know that harvest festival they're hosting the weekend after next?"

"Yeah."

"Katie and Roger had some volunteers bail on them," Marshal said. "And Sophie seems to think she'll have time to set up hay bales and pumpkin carving tables between all the extra baking she's doing and regular cooking for the inn."

"Sounds like Sophie."

"I'm supplying the pumpkins for their pumpkin patch anyways, so I offered to pitch in. Beena and I are heading over there next Friday to get started," Marshal said, referring to his one and only farmhand.

"I'm supposed to be in Vancouver that Friday for work," Dylan replied. "But I am hoping to switch days or take it off. Miss Natalie here has a birthday supper that evening."

"Yeah!" Natalie chimed in. "I'll be six!"

"Six!" Marshal replied. "You won't be a sprout anymore."

"See, Uncle Dylan?"

"Ha! We'll see how tall you get between now and then." He adjusted the rear-view mirror and gave her a wink. "I don't think I have any formal meetings that day, so it shouldn't be a problem with my boss. I'll let you know what he says."

"Great." Marshal sounded relieved. "I gotta run and get this delivery to the inn, but I'll let Katie know I have help. We can talk about it more Friday night. You still coming?"

"I don't know, every time I come over there you make me work. For free. Loading potatoes, usually—"

"See you then. Around seven."

"Got it."

With a click, the call disconnected.

Dylan turned onto a quiet street lined with red maple trees shedding their leaves in the mid-afternoon sun. An apartment complex sat across from a park filled with kids and parents watching from the sidelines. He pulled into its parking lot, then hopped out and unbuckled Natalie.

Seconds later, Justine pulled in and parked next to them. She got out, wearing yoga pants beneath her fall jacket, and approached them. Her thick black hair was pulled into a tight bun from her shift at the hospital.

Natalie bounded to her and hugged her around the waist. "Hi, Mom!"

Dylan gathered Natalie's backpack and mittens and gave the vehicle one last glance to make sure she hadn't left anything behind.

"Hey, baby." Justine hugged her daughter back, then looked at Dylan. "Thank you for picking her up again." She shook her head. "I don't know what we'll do when you're gone."

Natalie twisted to look up at him. "Yeah, we don't want you to go!"

His stomach pinched with guilt, and he handed Justine the pink backpack. "I don't want to move either, kiddo. But we'll see what happens." He glanced at Justine. "I'm still working on my boss to extend our remote agreement." *Who's refusing to get back to me.* Dylan didn't need to tell them that, though.

Natalie tugged her mom's sleeve. "I see Emma and Oliver at the park, is it okay if I go over there?"

"I was going to run to the store for pizza for tonight's supper. Why don't you load your stuff in the car and wait for me there? Your Nintendo is on the back seat," she said. "You can play your Paw Patrol game for a few minutes."

"Alright, I guess. See ya, Uncle Dylan."

"See ya, Sapling."

She flashed him a grin, then took her backpack from her mom and went to the backseat of her car.

"Thanks again," Justine said. "We still good for next Wednesday?"

Dylan nodded and closed the door of his SUV. "You bet." He paused. "Have you seen Mom recently? Or noticed her acting weird?"

"Weirder than usual?" Justine asked with an amused look.

He shoved his hands in his coat pockets. "Yeah. Like seeing Dad in the living room?"

She leaned toward him, her tone gentle. "Your mom's still grieving. I know it's been two years, but she spent thirty years of her life with him. And Ryan—" she paused. "Well, there's days I swear I can feel him here too. Especially around Natalie."

Dylan gave her a sideways look. "Right…"

She laughed and swatted his arm. "What's the harm in her reminiscing? She misses him. Let her heal in her own way."

He cleared this throat, pushing away the familiar ache in his chest. Thoughts of his childhood camping trips with his family—roughing it on overnight hikes in tents and sleeping bags—filled his mind. His brother's wide-eyed grin when they saw their first grizzly bear on the trail and slipped away scot-free. It was the same look he had at the altar when he married Justine, and at the hospital when Natalie was born—as if he'd been let in on life's greatest miracles.

And just like that, in one swift moment on a drive home from a father-son camping trip, he was gone. *They* were gone. And Dylan was supposed to be with them, but work had gotten in the way, as usual. He'd never forgiven himself for it—missing that last chance to spend time with them in the woods. Quality time, bonding time. Since his dad's remission, he'd thought they'd been given another chance. That his dad had been given another lease on life.

It wasn't fair to any of them—*but who said life is fair?*

"You okay?" Justine asked, pulling him back to the moment.

Dylan flicked his gaze to hers. "Yeah. You bet. See you next week."

"Sounds good. And don't forget about *somebody's* birthday next Friday." Justine jerked her head toward the car where Natalie sat inside, absorbed in her game.

"Couldn't forget. I have her pink unicorn glitter-bomb wrapped and ready to go."

"Ha ha." Justine rolled her eyes and got in her car.

First Mom's seeing Dad, now Justine's sensing Ryan around. He waved goodbye and jumped in his Explorer. *What a bunch of woo-woo BS.* He snorted. *But if it gives them comfort, what's the harm? I guess.*

He pulled out onto the street, then after a few intersections he headed down Main Street. He'd always admired the historic feel of the town—from the red brick buildings, to the vibrant dogwood trees that lined the street, and the metal benches beneath them. Cedar Lake was home to him. It always would be.

Valley Roast stood ahead at the end of the block, its rustic wood sign hanging over the door with a steaming cup of coffee painted on it. Dylan glanced at the clock on his dash. Three o'clock, plenty of time to grab a coffee before his daily virtual check-in with Jason.

Just as he was about to pull into an empty spot in front of the café, an old, blue rust-bucket coming from the other direction turned in front of him and stole the spot.

He slammed on his breaks, cursing under his breath. "Watch it!"

The car's door swung open and out stepped a pretty brunette in brown leather boots and a burgundy wool jacket. She looked up, and their gazes met—*Madison*.

Dylan's face softened, and he gave her a wry smile.

Her eyes widened. She cringed apologetically and mouthed, "Sorry!", then dashed into the coffee shop.

That girl. Always a walking cyclone.

He parked on the other side of the street and made his way inside. The mouth-watering smell of freshly roasted coffee and baked goods wafted over him. Since the after-work rush hadn't started yet, only a few tables were taken. Madison was the only person in line, waiting for the clerk to take her order.

Dylan shoved his keys in his coat pocket and joined her at the till. With a nervous grin, he cleared his throat. "We've got to stop meeting like this."

She glanced over her shoulder and gave him a wary look. "Like what?"

"Like you literally crashing into me."

She blinked. "I didn't. This time."

He cocked a brow. "I'd call that a near miss. Except this time something a lot more expensive than a cake box would have taken the hit."

"I'm sorry." Her cheeks reddened, and she raked her fingers through her long waves. "I didn't mean to cut you off. My mind's a little preoccupied lately."

"It's okay. Things happen." *Things like me ghosting her and breaking her heart?* His chest tightened. *I was just a kid,* he reminded himself. *Maybe I can make it up to her. At least we could be on friendly terms, now that she's back.*

She cast him a grateful look, her cheeks still pink.

A teenage boy with shaggy blond hair approached the till. He wore a name tag that read *Brody*. "Hi there, what can I get for you?"

Madison glanced at the chalkboard menu behind the till. "A large London fog, please. And a large chai latté with oat milk."

"I didn't know you could milk oats." Dylan winced at his own words. *Dad jokes? Really?*

Brody gave him an annoyed look, and Madison wrinkled her nose. "Good one."

He shifted uneasily, his neck warm. *I can do better than this, what's wrong with me?* "You're not one of those vegans now, are you?"

He bit back a groan. *Smooth. Real smooth.*

Madison met his gaze, a smile on the corner of her lips. "It's better than a steady diet of pizza and nachos—something I recall a certain boy from my past living on." She paused. "But no, the chai is for my mom. She's lactose intolerant."

Brody tapped the register impatiently, then gestured to the display screen. "That'll be ten seventy-five."

She reached for her hip where her non-existent purse should be, and her face dropped. "Darn it! I left my purse in my car." She glanced at the clerk. "Just one second, I'll run out and grab it."

"No problem," Brody replied. "I'll hang onto your drinks until you get back."

"I'll get it." Dylan offered. He took out his wallet and opened it.

"Oh, that's okay, you don't have to."

"My way of making up for the other day. For making you drop your cake."

Madison tilted her head. "That was one of my own graceful moves."

"Look, I never get to be a knight in shining armour," Dylan replied. "Usually, I'm like… the stable boy getting yelled at by his boss. You'll be doing my self-esteem a favour."

Madison crossed her arms, her eyes bright as she swept him with her intense gaze.

He flashed her a cheesy smile. One that had once worked to melt her hard exterior, back when they were teens. "I need this. For my pride."

"I think you should just let him do it," Brody said. "He owes you after that terrible joke."

Madison let out a sigh. "Fine. I guess I can play a damsel in distress if it'll make you feel better."

"Thank you." Dylan pulled out twenty and handed it to Brody. "Add a large black coffee and one of your raisin bran muffins to that. No worries about the change."

"Got it." Brody tipped his head and left to gather their drinks.

"Raisin bran? I take back what I said about the pizza. Glad to see you've added some fibre to your diet," Madison quipped, then uncrossed her arms. "Sorry, I didn't mean to be mean. Thanks for getting this for me. I owe you."

For a moment, her expression warmed. She looked at him the same way she did ten years ago, with that easy smile—as if no time had passed. As if he hadn't left her, and she hadn't married somebody else. Dylan's stomach knotted. He almost slipped back to his eighteen-year-old self, bantering with his girlfriend.

He swallowed. "I'll hold you to that. Next time, you can buy." *Next time*? He rubbed the back of his neck. "I mean—"

Brody returned holding two large cups. "Here's the drinks for the damsel no longer in distress."

Madison took them from him, then looked at Dylan. "Next time, I'll make sure I don't cut you off with my car." She tipped her head. "Thanks again. I better run this to Mom before it gets cold."

"Right. Of course." Dylan leaned back on his heels. "See you Friday at Marshal's?"

She hesitated, then gave him a nervous smile. "Sure thing. See you then."

Dylan's gaze trailed after her as she made her way to the door, shouldered it open, and disappeared outside. *Well, that was awkward. But I think we ended on okay terms.* The thought of her light-hearted teasing eased the tension from his shoulders. *And really, that's all I can ask for. With everything going on—her divorce, my stupid job situation, my mom and Justine believing they're haunted—neither of us need any more complications. Definitely no dredging up the past.*

Brody returned and set a paper cup on the counter. "Here's your coffee. Do you want your muffin to go?"

"Sure," Dylan replied. "Can you add a chocolate chip cookie to that?"

Brody raised a brow. "Didn't want her to see you buying junk food?"

Dylan pressed his lips together. *I don't even like raisins. Or bran.* "No, it's not that."

"Sure." Brody snorted and turned to the back to grab him his cookie.

Chapter Five

Madison side-stepped into her parents' log house and closed the door with her butt. She lifted the hot drinks above her head to avoid the tawny monster of a dog bounding toward her with a white miniature poodle hot on his heels.

"Mack! Dolly! Sit!" she commanded.

Her leggy mutt skidded to a stop at her feet and planted his butt on the floor, his tail wriggling with barely-contained excitement. Dolly sat politely next to him, the top of her fluffy head barely reaching his shoulder.

"Good dogs," Madison cooed. "Now, wait."

She kicked off her boots and walked into the kitchen, keeping the dogs in the corner of her eye.

They both craned their necks to stare after her, but stayed put. After setting the drinks on the granite counter next to the sink, she opened the cupboard and pulled out two treats.

"Alright," she said, facing the dogs. "Come!"

Dolly sprang up and dashed to Madison's side. Mack lunged to his feet and turned like a bull in a china shop, narrowly missing the coat rack by the door, and galloped to join her.

"Good dogs." Madison had them sit once more, then gave them their treats. "I missed you guys today. But I got to see some other good boys and girls who needed the love."

She'd gone into Pawsitive Match that afternoon to talk to Danica about the fundraiser at Starlight Inn's harvest festival. Just as she had hoped, Danica agreed right away and was just as excited as Madison about it. She even had a few dogs in mind to bring over to take part and meet people, and one of them included Monty, whose affectionate attitude was sure to win some prospective new owner's heart. Madison's heart squeezed at the thought of him finding a forever home in time for the holidays.

Mack snuffled her pockets, looking for more treats, and Madison scratched his ears. "Sorry, bud. That's it for now. Once Mom gets home, we'll go out for a walk."

Which is one nice thing about home—the trails. Her parents' log house sat on a small acreage that backed onto Cedar Lake. They had access to the trail around the lake right from their backyard, just a quick jaunt down some steps through the trees. She hadn't paid much attention to the beauty of this place when she was a kid. Now, compared to the apartment condo she had shared with Jamie, it was like heaven. And Mack definitely seemed to agree.

She took a sip of her London fog, enjoying the sweet vanilla flavour. *I can't believe I left my purse in the car. And Dylan*—she shook her head, smiling at the thought of their exchange. This time, he'd been the one caught off guard. It didn't matter that her heart had been beating faster than a hummingbird's wings. She'd kept her cool and made a step in the right direction to get back into the flow of this town.

She leaned her hip on the counter, gazing out the window at her parents' perfectly manicured lawn.

Despite backing onto the treed section of the lake, there wasn't a single leaf marring the freshly mowed grass. The stone patio had been swept clean, not a pine cone in sight. This acreage was her father's pride and joy. He put as much care into it as he did his patients at his clinic in town.

Her gaze landed on the fire pit at the centre of the patio, and her thoughts shifted to Marshal's gathering on Friday. *Maybe it won't be so hard. If I can avoid nosy questions and smooth things over with Dylan like I did today, I'm sure I can do it with everyone else.*

She set her drink on the counter and chewed the side of her cheek. *I wonder what he meant by "next time"?* Her heart rate quickened. *Probably just being friendly. I mean, he's buddies with Marshal. We're going to see each other around. It's better for everybody if we get along. And revisiting our past would only bring up bad feelings.* She nodded to herself. It was time for a fresh start. With Dylan, with this town, with her whole life.

The door opened and Madison's mom stepped inside. In a mad dash of barks and scrambling paws, the dogs bounded toward her. She hung her purse on the coat rack and checked her cropped grey hair in the mirror before turning to the dogs with a wide smile.

"Sit!"

Mack nudged her arm with his nose. Dolly stood on her hind legs, begging for attention.

"Oh all right, you two deserve all the love." She gave them each a good ear scratch, then kicked off her heels and fished her runners out from beneath the log bench by the door. "Hey, Madi. How was your day?"

"It was so good!" Madison grabbed the two Valley Roast cups from the counter and made her way to the entrance. "I met with Danica and everything's a go for the fundraiser." She paused, thinking of all the lonely dogs waiting for homes. "It's going to be such a great thing for both Pawsitive Match and the Starlight Inn."

"Happy to hear you're excited about something." Paula finished tying her shoes and straightened, then grabbed Dolly's pink leash from one of the hooks above the bench. "It's important to stay busy when you're going through something like this. It keeps you from wallowing."

Madison's stomach clenched. For the first time since she left Vancouver, she'd hardly thought about her divorce at all that day. She swallowed the thought and gave her mom a tight smile. "Yeah, totally. Thought I could pick your brain about event planning tonight?"

"Oh, I've done nothing but event organization all day." Paula sighed and clipped her leash to Dolly's pink harness. "We're already in the thick of planning the town hall Christmas Tree Lighting. They want to have a market this year. Dealing with vendors is a nightmare."

"Come on, Mom. I bought you a chai latté." Madison held it out to her. "Well, I guess technically Dylan bought it—"

Her mom's gaze shot to hers, her piercing blue eyes narrowed. She took the cup from Madison with stiff fingers. "Dylan? Dylan Stewart?"

Crap. Madison bit back a groan. *Why did I bring him up?* "I forgot my purse in my car at Valley Roast, and he was in line behind me and offered to pay. It was nothing, really. Just a quick hi and a nice gesture."

"That boy owes you more than a nice gesture."

Paula huffed and checked the zipper on her jacket. "The last thing you need is another heartbreak. I'd steer clear of him, if I were you."

"I'm not stupid, Mom." Madison cringed. Dylan wasn't exactly on her parents' good list. Luckily, after the trip cancellation, they'd been able to get a refund on Madison's flights. But they'd still had to deal with her emotional fall-out. Which, at eighteen, had been pretty dramatic.

Her neck grew warm, and guilt washed over her. *And now they have to deal with it all over again. Except worse.* Avoiding her mom's gaze, she balanced her drink in one hand and slipped on her runners.

Paula clucked her tongue and gave Madison a soft look. "I know that, dear. You're very smart. But sometimes, you don't make the best decisions when it comes to your heart—"

"Mom!" Madison snatched Mack's leather leash off the hook and snapped it onto the ring on his harness. "You think I don't know that? The last thing I'm looking for right now is *romance*."

"Have you been to see that counselor I suggested yet?"

"Don't change the subject."

"Well, have you?" Paula tipped her cup in Madison's direction. "She would really help you work on your feelings about men—"

"I went once, okay?" Madison replied, heat rising through her chest. It hadn't exactly been the most successful session. They'd barely scratched the surface of what was going on inside her, and Madison hadn't been able to lower that sky-high wall she had built around herself. "She gave me some journaling prompts to work through. Because you know, since I can't speak my feelings," she raised her voice to imitate the counselor, "maybe I can write my inner child a self-love letter."

"Have you tried doing it yet?"

Madison made a fake gagging nose. "No. You think that stuff really works?"

Paula looped Dolly's leash over her forearm. "Dr. Theresa is a professional counsellor with a masters in Social Work, specializing in domestic abuse. If she says it works, it probably does." She reached out and squeezed Madison's shoulder. "I just want you to feel better. Get your head on straight. What Jamie did—"

"Was horrible," Madison cut her off. "I know. I'll go back to Dr. Theresa, if you think it'll help." Mack nudged her elbow with his soft nose, and she cleared her throat. "Now, let's get going. These dogs have been cooped up all day."

Paula gave her a sideways glance. "Alright, I'll back off. For now." She opened the door and gestured for Madison to go first. "Now, tell me about this fundraiser. You said before that you're going to offer family photos?"

Madison stepped outside with Mack plodding along beside her. "Yep. In the pumpkin patch. It's going to be such a cute set-up."

Paula followed with Dolly and closed the door. "I wonder if I can get Matthew home for some family photos," she said, referring to Madison and Marshal's younger brother. "I doubt he'd come in time for the festival, but maybe he'll be here for some Christmas pictures. We haven't seen him since your father and I flew out to Toronto in July to visit him." She frowned. "And he hasn't answered my calls for weeks."

"I'm sure he's just busy, living it up with Brittany," Madison replied, referring to her brother's girlfriend.

Two years ago, he'd landed an editing job at a small publishing house in Toronto. Shortly after moving he'd met Brittany, an ambitious intern, and they'd been solid ever since. "You know how those kids are—"

"He's only two years younger than you and Marsh."

"Well, he still looks like a baby. Did he have any sign of a single facial hair yet?"

The two wound their way down to the entrance of the path, Madison feeling better. Her thoughts wandered to her conversation with Dylan in Valley Roast, and their promise of *next time*. Maybe her mom had a point. Maybe trying to be friends with Dylan would just add more emotional complications to her life—which was the absolute last thing she needed.

She began the decline down the cut-in steps in the hill toward the lake trail, Mack tugging at his harness in front of her. Her mom and Dolly walked carefully in front of her, Paula chattering about the hayrides at the inn.

I'll talk to Dylan on Friday. Set things right. We'll strictly be friendly acquaintances, nothing more.

Late that evening, Madison sat cross-legged on the floor of her basement bedroom surrounded by cardboard boxes. She'd slipped into her favourite flannel pajamas and loosely braided her hair for bed, and it now fell over her shoulder as she rifled through the contents of the nearest box.

In the three weeks that she'd been home, she hadn't had the energy to even think about unpacking more than the essentials—her toiletries, a few changes of clothes, and Mack's things. She didn't have much more than that, anyways. Not anymore. She'd only been able to take her personal belongings when she left. Mack's kennel. Books. A few old movies. Her jewelry and a few trinkets from her grandmother. So much of the life she'd built had been left behind.

Mack snorted in his sleep, sprawled in his fluffy bed in the corner. Once she settled in for the night, he would probably jump on her bed and join her, taking up almost as much room as she did. A few weeks ago, she'd never have allowed it. *Or rather, Jamie would never have allowed it.* He'd rarely even let Mack off his cushion, much less on the furniture. Now, Madison couldn't get enough of the dog's comfort.

As if sensing her pain, he always came to her when she cried and would nestle his head in her lap. Or snuffle her hair. *Or decide he's a poodle and squeeze his big butt in my lap.*

Her heart pricked as she gazed at the dog. *I can't believe I let Jamie treat him so terribly. Like an object instead of the living, breathing, pure-hearted creature he is.* Disgust roiled inside her. Shame that she hadn't protected her dog more. *What is wrong with me? I don't deserve Mack. Or even Mom and Dad. The number of times Jamie was rude to them...* Memories of him sulking at family get-togethers, his bushy brows knit together in his typical scowl, swam in her mind.

Stop thinking about it. I'm away from him now. He can't hurt my family or Mack ever again. She blinked back a tear, then opened the box in front of her. The pearl-white fabric of her wedding dress, scrunched up and shoved in the box as if it were burlap and not delicate lace, greeted her.

She slammed the box closed and kicked it to the side. *Nope. I'm not doing this. Not tonight.* She let out a breath and tucked a stray lock of hair behind her ear, then got to her feet and opened her closet.

She stacked all four boxes inside, put her hands on her hips, and glared at them. "I don't even want to look at you yet."

Just as she was about to close the door, a glint of red from the top shelf caught her eye. *Is that what I think it is?* She stood on her toes and pulled the cranberry-coloured shoe box down. She wiped the dust from the top and popped open the lid.

Her heart hitched. *Holy smokes.*

Scattered notes in her and Sophie's handwriting from high school lay inside it. Pink hearts, lop-sided stars, and goofy messages with quotes from their favourite movies. A photo of the girls and Madison's brothers sitting around a campfire when they were maybe thirteen or fourteen years old. There was a worn, beaded friendship bracelet Sophie had made for her that she'd lost in the Johnsons' backyard pool, but Lily Johnson had found it clogged in one of the pool drains and returned it to her. Ticket stubs from the first Canucks game she and her brothers went to with their dad.

She shifted aside a folded paper fortune-teller with purple flowers doodled on it, and there it was.

A photo of her and Dylan at their Junior High graduation, a full two years before they ever dated. Dylan's suit was loose on his lean frame, and her purple velvet dress reminded her way too much of her grandmother's old couch cushions. But the way he gazed at her through his then-floppy bangs, and her wide grin despite the braces she had hated so much—*that spark*. They'd always had it.

She picked up the picture with trembling fingers and turned it over to read the note on the back.

Hey Mads, remember this? When you tripped on your heels walking onto the stage and almost took me down with you? That's when I knew. He'd doodled a heart at the bottom.

Madison's throat thickened, and she gently placed the photo back in the box. He'd given it to her for her birthday a few years later, before everything had gone downhill. Before his dad got sick, and his walls went up.

Why am I even looking at this? Another thing I can't deal with tonight. She placed the red box on the top of her old bookcase across from her bed, then tiptoed around Mack and slid beneath her covers, her heart thumping against her ribs.

As usual, Mack snorted and clambered into bed with her, then flopped down on top of the blankets on her other side. He let out a yawn and stretched out his long legs, gazing at her through half-closed lids.

"You're such a goof." She scratched his ear, then rolled over to turn off the lamp on her bedside table. The flowered journal her counselor had given her lay next to the light, and her mother's words from earlier that day echoed in her mind.

"Okay. I'll give it a go." She sat up and grabbed the notebook and the pen that lay next to it and flipped it open. She skimmed the counselor's instructions about how to use the guided entries, then turned to the first page.

Day One - List ten things that light you up.

Really? Madison stifled a groan. *I have to try. For Mom.*

She thought for a moment, then lowered her pen to the paper with trembling fingers. *Old memories and lifelong friends.*

CHAPTER SIX

Dylan drummed his fingers on his steering wheel, sullenly listening to Jingle Bells pouring from the speaker of his phone. *It's October, why are they playing Christmas carols as hold music already?*

It was Friday evening and he was parked in his mother's driveway, waiting for his boss to get back on the phone before he went inside. He'd called Jason to make sure he could take next Friday off, and Jason had left him on hold for almost ten minutes already.

His mom had called him while he was driving back to Cedar Lake from his meeting at the office in Vancouver. Apparently, her Wi-Fi wasn't working, so he decided to pop by on his way out to Marshal's.

Jason's voice cut off the song in his ear. "Dylan, you still there?"

"Sure am."

"I finally heard back from Ken," he said, referring to his manager. "He said it's fine if you'd like to take next Friday off."

"Thanks, Jason." He paused, thinking of the email he sent on Wednesday asking about an extension on his work-from-home privileges. "Any word on the workplace situation come January?"

Jason hesitated. "Look, Dylan. We really appreciate your work. You're one of our best, and we want to keep you happy. But we're expanding and going to need you in here more often with these projects starting up—"

"I'm willing to drive in twice a week, if that's what it takes."

"You know Ken hates the virtual meetings. He's old school. He likes having his team together."

Old school? Not exactly the best mindset for the tech industry. "So that's a no?"

Jason sighed. "No firm answer yet. I'm working on him. I'll throw the twice a week idea at him and see if he bites."

"Thanks, Jason."

"See you online on Monday."

Dylan hung up, then got out of his Explorer and started up his mom's steps. The faint sound of soft, flowy music met his ears, but the lights inside were dimmed.

That's weird. What's she up to? His stomach knotted. The last time he'd found her sitting in the dark, she'd been watching some silly romance movie and crying because it reminded her of his father.

He knocked on the door, and a chorus of giggles sounded from the other side. He cracked it open. "Mom?"

"We're in the living room, dear. Come on in," she called out.

Dylan let himself in, and the music became clearer. Slow and peaceful, it reminded him of something his massage therapist played in the waiting area. He scratched his chin. *Is that wind chimes?*

He stepped through the doorway and into the dark living room. The deep, woody scent of sandalwood wafted over him. His mom and Christine Walsh sat cross-legged, facing each other in the middle of the floor.

A phone, a lit candle, a bowl of incense, and a deck of cards with moons and stars on the back sat between them. The coffee table had been pushed up against the couch to give them room. And the ugliest stone angel he'd ever seen stood on top of it, looking over them with roughly carved eyes. Its wings were chipped and worn, one of them marred with a jagged crack.

What in the name of all things holy is that? He tried to hide his grimace.

Christine gave him a cheeky smile, the candlelight dancing across her grey-streaked red waves that hung to her waist. "Hello, Dylan. How are you?"

Do I even want to know what's going on here? Dylan gave the soulless angel a side-eye, then cleared his throat. "I'm good, Christine. How are you?"

"Just peachy, thanks."

Peachy. He gave her an amused look. How did Sophie come from this woman? *She'd never be caught dead having some kind of séance—or whatever it is they're doing.*

"So, Mom, you need help with your internet?"

His mom craned her neck to look up at him, a purple shawl with gold tassels strewn over her shoulders.

"Yes, dear. For some reason we can't get Christine's phone to connect to the Wi-Fi. I checked mine, and it's not working either."

She picked up the phone, got to her feet, and walked over to him. After turning the sound off, she thrust the device under his nose. "See? No bars. We're trying to cleanse the negative energy in here with this music from Christine's playlist, but I'm afraid we're using up her data."

Cleansing negative energy? He hooked his thumb at the angel. "Get rid of that. Problem solved."

Christine raised her brows. "Excuse me?"

"That thing's got to be emitting *negative energy* like radio waves."

"It's an angel," Cathy said.

"An evil one?"

Christine snorted a laugh.

His Mom wiggled the phone in his face. "Could you stop joking for a second and take a look?"

He took the phone from her, softening at her red cheeks and misty eyes. His chest twinged. *She's upset. Why is she upset?* "Sorry, Mom. I didn't mean anything by it."

He glanced at the phone, handed it back to her, and made his way to the TV stand and the overfilled power bar behind it. He knelt down and began to sort through the cords. "I'm going to restart your router. We'll see if that fixes the connection."

He found the right one, unplugged it, waited a few seconds, then plugged it back in. "Let's wait a couple minutes for it to reboot." He paused. "I'll grab you another power bar from home and bring it over this weekend. This thing," he gestured toward the tangled mess of cords, "has got to be a safety hazard."

"Thanks, dear. I appreciate that." Cathy sat down across from Christine, gazing at the phone's screen. She glanced at her friend. "Energy flow—is that the right playlist?"

Christine began to shuffle the cards. "Sure. Or you could try Interstellar. That's a nice one I made for Tina's reading."

Dylan got to his feet, shifting uncomfortably in the silence. *Dare I ask?* "So, what are you ladies up to tonight, exactly?"

His mom lifted her chin. "Christine is doing a tarot reading for me."

"A tarot reading?" He furrowed his brows. *Why?* "Okay. Cool."

"I know you don't believe in this stuff," Cathy said, meeting his eye. "But it helps me. It gives me some guidance, makes me feel more connected."

Dylan swallowed the lump in his throat. Instead of cracking his usual joke, he chose his words carefully. "I think it's good for you to do whatever makes you happy."

Still, he couldn't fight the tug of guilt in the back of his mind. *Is she scared because I'm leaving? Is that why she's doing all this? For comfort?*

"Besides," Christine said, setting the cards down in a neat pile. "It's fun."

"Exactly." Cathy pointed at the deck. "Want to pull one? Just for kicks?"

Dylan gave her a dry look. "Check the phone. Is it connected yet?"

His mom squinted at her phone and gave it a swipe. "Yes! Thanks, hon. I appreciate it." She tapped at the screen, and the flowy music started again. "Care to stick around, or are you headed out on the town?"

"I haven't been *out on the town* for years." He fought the urge to roll his eyes. "But I am going to Marshal's, so I should head out."

"Sophie mentioned Marshal was having a fire tonight." Christine picked up the incense bowl and wafted the smoke from it over the cards. "She also said Madison's coming. I guess she's back in town."

Dylan's throat went dry. *Those gossipers.* He bet Sophie told her about their bump-in at the inn. He shoved his hands in his pockets and tried to make his face passive. "Is that so?"

"Madison Talbot?" Cathy's voice sounded surprised. "Paula and Bill never liked that man she married. I wonder what happened. You know," she glanced at Dylan, "she was always such a nice girl. I always thought you were meant to be together. You never told me why you two ended things."

He edged toward the door, his back stiff. "I told you, we drifted apart. Like most kids do when they go off to college."

She gave him a sad look. "You two had that trip all planned out—"

"Mom," he said. "It was ten years ago. It's fine.

In fact, I saw her the other day at Valley Roast, and it was just—well, fine."

His mom and Christine exchanged knowing smiles.

Christine set down the incense bowl. "Sophie always said you two were perfect together."

He shook his head, now standing in the entryway to the kitchen. "Don't get any thoughts in your heads about us." His neck grew hot. "She just got away from a huge jerk. She doesn't need another one in her life."

He cringed. *That came out harsher than I meant.*

"Dylan!"

"I didn't mean it like that." He ran his hand through his hair and let out a flustered sigh. "Besides, Mom, you know my life is up in the air right now. It's not exactly the best timing for me to start dating anybody."

"It's not like Vancouver is that far," Cathy pointed out. "Madison coming back, it could be a sign—"

"Look, you ladies have fun tonight playing with your cards. I've gotta get going. It's almost seven."

His mom threw her hands in the air with a look of resignation, then got to her feet and gave him a hug. "Okay, dear. Have fun. And if anything happens with Madison—"

"It won't." He hugged her back, then looked again at their whole weird set up. Christine smiled serenely, and he could have sworn that creepy angel was staring at him. "Are you sure you're doing okay, Mom?"

"Of course," she replied. "I haven't felt this good in years."

"If you need anything," he paused, "or if you see dad again, give me a call."

"I'm fine, dear." Cathy patted his arm, her jovial demeanour back in place. "Really. And if I see your father, I'll tell him you say hi."

"Funny," he replied.

"Wait." Christine held up her hand, a mischievous glint in her eye. "Before you go, let me draw you a card. I have a strong feeling there's a message here for you."

"Ah, come on, Christine. I don't—"

"Oh, Dylan. Humour her!" His mom waved her hand toward her friend.

"Fine."

Christine closed her eyes, then cut the cards and pulled one from the top of the second stack. She flipped it over, then showed it to him with a smug look.

The candlelight flickered across glossy painted artwork of a naked man and woman holding hands in a garden.

"The Lovers," she said. "A relationship card! Love, values, harmony, and most importantly—making the right choices about them." She cocked her head dramatically. "Seems timely, doesn't it?"

Dylan barked a laugh. "Are you saying I'm going to meet my soulmate tonight? With my luck, it's probably Marshal."

Christine returned the card to the pile, a hint of a smile on her lips. "Maybe think about the choices part, hmm?"

Dylan waved them off. "I'm out of here before things get any weirder. You ladies enjoy your evening with your messed-up angel."

Both women went into a fit of giggles and waved him off.

He made his way outside to his vehicle, shaking his head. *The Lovers. What a bunch of nonsense.*

The memory of Madison and her mischievous smile in Valley Roast floated into his mind. She did look good. And she seemed happy. *But still, it would never work.*

I blew my chance with her ten years ago. And with everything going on in each of our lives, the timing couldn't be worse.

He thought of Christine's tarot card, *the Lovers*, and bit back a laugh. *There's no such thing as soulmates, anyways. That's for sure.*

CHAPTER SEVEN

Madison swirled the iced ginger ale around in her plastic cup, then set it down on the fold-out table Marshal had set up near the fire pit in his backyard. She shoved her cold fingers in the pockets of her down vest. The sun had just gone down, leaving a sharp bite in the autumn air. The crackling fire warmed her back, beckoning her to join the group that sat around it.

Beside her, Sophie popped the plastic cover off the tray she'd just set on the table. Miniature cupcakes with caramel-coloured icing and orange sprinkles sat inside.

"You are the only person I know who'd bring cupcakes to a bonfire," Madison said.

Sophie picked one up and handed it to her. "I have a reputation to uphold. And bringing potato chips to a get-together isn't it. These are a new recipe—maple sugar cupcakes. What do you think?"

"If they're sugary, I'll love them." Madison peeled the cupcake liner from the pastry and took a bite. The heavy flavour of maple with hints of vanilla and caramel practically melted in her mouth. "Oh my goodness, Sophie! Please tell me you're making these for the harvest festival."

Sophie clasped her hands, a gleeful look on her face. "They're that good?"

Madison tossed the liner into the garbage next to the table, then popped the rest of the treat into her mouth. "They're delicious."

"I hope the others like them. Because yes, I am definitely testing them tonight for the fundraiser sale at the festival. I mean, Marshal loves them. But he's biased." Sophie helped herself to one of the bite-sized cupcakes. "Speaking of the festival, Katie told me you got Pawsitive Match on board. Good work."

"Yeah, Danica was thrilled with the idea."

Madison's heart lifted. "We're going to set up a booth with photos of the shelter and information about all the available pets and how to volunteer or donate, plus we'll bring four of the calmer dogs for meet-and-greets. I think they'll draw a lot of attention."

"That sounds perfect! Are you coming to the committee meeting on Saturday?" Sophie asked. "You'll get to meet Rodger, Katie's husband, and all the Starlight Inn gang."

"Yeah, Katie told me about it. One o'clock, right? I'll be there."

"Yay! I'm so glad you're hopping on board."

A guy who looked to be in his early twenties approached the table. "Hey, Sophie. Those the maple-sugars you told me about?" The firelight flickered across his russet-brown skin, catching his relaxed smile.

"They sure are." Sophie gestured to the tray. "Help yourself. Madison, you remember Tad, right? You met him when you and Marshal dropped off those pumpkins."

Madison nodded, thinking back to that crazy day. It was the day she'd left Jamie, and Marshal had come to Vancouver to help her move home.

He'd been in a panic to find sugar pumpkins for Sophie to use for catering a wedding that weekend. On the way home, they had stopped at a pumpkin patch farm to get Sophie the goods. It had been a nice distraction from that afternoon's emotional chaos.

"Hey, Tad. That was a strange day for me. Sorry if I came off as weird."

Tad shrugged and grabbed a cupcake from the tray. "You didn't come off as weird. A little enthusiastic about pumpkins, maybe. But after hanging out with Sophie all day for the last few months, produce-passion is nothing new to me."

"Where's Ethan?" Sophie asked, referring to one of the stable hands at the inn. "You two have been spending a lot of time together. I thought he'd be here."

Tad bit into the cupcake and chewed for a second, then swallowed. "He had other plans tonight, apparently. Plans that didn't involve me."

"Oh, I'm sorry." Sophie reached out and squeezed his forearm.

"It's fine," Tad said in a way that told Madison it really wasn't. He finished the cupcake, then licked the icing from his lips. "These are amazing, by the way. Perfect for a fall-themed festival."

"Stay tuned for the pumpkin muffins this weekend at the committee meeting," Sophie replied.

"I'm sure they'll be fantastic, like everything you make." He nodded toward the group of people around the bonfire. "Anna just got here," he said, referring to another member of the kitchen staff at the inn. "I better go say hi."

"We'll be right behind you." Sophie gave him a wave. She turned to Madison and gestured toward some empty lawn chairs near the fire. "Shall we go sit and warm up? It's freezing over here."

Madison pressed her lips together, her attention back on the party. Marshal's *small gathering* had turned into a group of about twenty or so people. More than she'd expected, and she spotted a few people from high school she didn't feel ready to face. In the twenty-odd minutes she'd been there, she'd stuck to the fringes, helping Sophie set out food.

"I need to use the washroom first," Madison replied, her mouth dry. "Is the back door to Marshal's house open?"

"It should be." Sophie shivered and pulled her jacket tighter around her. She glanced at the icy drink Madison had placed on the table. "Do you want something hot to drink? It's way too chilly out. I could make us some tea."

Madison raised a brow. "Marshal has tea?"

"Earl Grey, Green, or Oolong," Sophie replied with a grin. "He keeps them in his coffee cupboard for me."

"Well, aren't you two stinking adorable." Madison gave her a lighthearted nudge with her elbow. *Marshal and Sophie,* she mused. She was still getting used to the idea of her brother dating her best friend. While Madison had always thought they'd had a spark, it had taken them years to discover it.

Probably better that way. I rushed things with Jamie and look how that turned out. She pushed the painful memory away, then thought of Dylan the other day in Valley Roast. The way his hair curled at the edges. His easy smile. Even his bad dad jokes were cute. *I wonder what would have happened if Dylan and I had waited to date? If we'd just been friends and let our feelings simmer, like Sophie and Marsh?*

Maybe they wouldn't have crashed and burned. Maybe she wouldn't have been so quick to hook up with Jamie to soothe her aching heart. *Stop it. What's done is done.*

"He's definitely one of a kind." Sophie looked across the fire at Marshal and gave him a little wave. He caught her gaze with a silly smile and waved back.

"Ugh. Barf, you two." Madison picked up her plastic cup and tossed it in the garbage. "Let's go get that tea."

"Fine, but you have to stop saying things like *barf* when referring to Marshal and me." Sophie hooked her arm through Madison's and bumped her with her hip playfully.

Dylan's voice came from behind them. "I think barf is an appropriate description when it comes to the way you two make googly eyes at each other."

Madison's chest tightened. She hesitated, then turned to face him, dragging Sophie with her. "Dylan! Hey."

He rocked back on his heels and gave them his signature carefree grin—the one that revealed the dimple in his chin. One hand was tucked in the pocket of his canvas jacket, and he held a red plastic cup with the other. "I hear there's some delicious homemade goodies over here."

"Not for you, after that comment," Sophie teased.

Marshal waved at Sophie again from his chair, then got to his feet. A couple Madison recognized from high school stood next to him. He gestured toward his shop on the other side of his driveway. "I'm going to show Mark and Isla here the new Kubota tractor, want to come with us?"

Sophie slid her gaze between Madison and Dylan, then gave Madison a nervous look. "You okay here if I tag along with them?"

Madison's stomach knotted, but she nodded. "I'm fine. I don't need babysitting. Pretty sure all the sharp objects have been put out of my reach."

Dylan pointed his drink toward the ax leaning against the stump beside the wood pile. "I'll steer her clear of that one too."

Madison snorted. "Trust me, if we run out of firewood, I won't be volunteering to chop more. Isn't that what you're here for?"

Dylan raised his brows with an amused look. Heat rushed to Madison's face. *And I fall right back into it, just like that.* He made it too easy to slip into old habits, as if they were still friends. As if they hadn't crashed against the rocks and vanished from each other's lives for ten years.

Sophie tilted her head and twirled one of her copper locks around her finger. "If you're sure…"

"I'm sure. Go." Madison pulled her arm from Sophie's.

"We shouldn't be long." Sophie cast her a reassuring look, then strode after Marshal and their friends toward the shop.

Madison hugged her elbows and glanced at Dylan from the corner of her eye, torn between making small-talk with him, taking a seat at the fire with the others, or rushing to her car to make a run for home.

He cleared his throat. "So, how was coffee with your mom?"

"Oh, good. I guess," she replied. "You know, I see her every day now, so it's not like it was anything special."

Smooth. Way to broadcast that I'm living at home now.

"Well, it was nice of you to get her something." He paused and gestured toward her with his cup. "Are you cold?"

Madison glanced down at her white-knuckled grip on her elbows. "Umm. Kind of. I was just going inside."

"Here." Dylan slipped off his canvas jacket, revealing a nicely fitted sweater, and held it out to her.

Madison swallowed and lifted a brow. "Well, aren't you the chivalrous one."

"I told you, the whole knight-in-shining-armour routine is for my own self-esteem." He stepped behind her and draped the jacket over her shoulders.

She glanced up at him, letting his warmth envelop her. She'd forgotten how tall he was, and how his mere presence used to make her feel safe and at home. The exact opposite of Jamie. She'd grown used to walking on eggshells every time her ex-husband walked into the room. As if it were normal to react that way to your supposed soulmate.

A hint of something earthy wafted over her. Before she could stop herself, she blurted out, "Is that *sandalwood*?"

Dylan groaned and took a step away from her. He lifted the collar of his sweater to his nose and sniffed. "Probably. I was just at Mom's and Christine was there, burning some type of incense."

"Sophie's mom?" Madison's lip twitched. "Sounds about right. Their house always smelled like a forest."

He let out a laugh, then gestured toward her empty hand. "Do you need something to drink? I have some stuff inside I could share with you."

"Oh, nope. I'm fine." Madison stiffened. She wriggled and shoved her arms through Dylan's oversized sleeves. "I don't drink at all anymore. My ex was an alcoholic, and I just can't."

"I don't either," Dylan replied. He held up his cup. "Non-alcoholic cider. I promise."

Madison tilted her head. "Really?"

"Well," he said slowly. "Since the accident a couple years ago, I just can't bring myself to—"

"What accident?"

He hesitated, his face drawn. "My dad and Ryan. That drunk driver." He cleared his throat. "We lost them. That's why I moved back here, for Mom. Marshal didn't tell you?"

Madison's heart slammed against her ribs. *They lost them?* Dylan's dad and brother were gone? *After how hard his dad fought to beat cancer*—her stomach lurched. "N-no. He didn't say anything. Dylan, I'm so sorry."

"I'm okay. It was two years ago—"

A high-pitched voice cut through their conversation.

"Madison Talbot? Is that you? I heard you'd moved back to Cedar Lake!"

Madison spun around. A leggy woman with long, perfectly curled blond hair strode toward her from the direction of the parking area next to Marshal's house. A man in a baggy hoodie with a box of beer under his arm followed behind her.

Madison's heart dropped. *Ashley Adams.* The biggest gossip from their class.

"Ashley, hey." *Come on, Madison. Give her the benefit of the doubt. Maybe she's changed.*

But the way Ashley flicked her gaze from Madison to Dylan, a wicked grin forming on her ruby red lips, told Madison everything she needed to know.

Ashley stopped in front of them, her hands on her hips. "Is it true you're living at home? And are you two—" she pointed back and forth between Madison and Dylan with a perfectly manicured finger— "dating again?"

Madison bit back a groan, fighting the urge to dash to her car and take off.

Great. Just great. Exactly what I was trying to avoid.

CHAPTER EIGHT

Dylan's stomach hardened at Ashley's words. He glanced at Madison, waiting for her usual witty comeback, but the ashen look on her face said it all—Ashley had struck a nerve.

Why did that busybody have to butt in? Right now, when the ice between Madison and I was beginning to thaw?

"Well?" Ashley demanded, tapping her boot against the ground. "Are you two together again or what?"

Madison's face grew even paler. "I, uh—"

Dylan cleared his throat. "Hey, Ashley. If we're playing twenty questions, I've got one for you."

Ashley stared at him. "Excuse me?"

"That's what you're doing, right? Twenty questions?" Dylan replied dryly. "My turn." He held her gaze. "Is it socially acceptable to put somebody you haven't seen for years on the spot with inappropriate questions?"

Ashley scowled, then flipped her blond curls behind her shoulder. "Whatever, Dylan. Why are you always so confrontational?"

Her boyfriend, whom Dylan recognized from Marshal's summer slo-pitch team, caught up to her and put his arm around her waist. "Come on, Ash. Let's go sit." He dipped his head toward Dylan. "Hey, Dylan."

"Hey, Brian."

Ashley cast Dylan a wary glance, then turned to Madison. "Well, it's nice to see you out and about. I'm sure we'll catch up later."

Madison shifted Dylan's jacket around her shoulders. "Yeah. Sure. Sometime."

Ashley gave Dylan another dark look, then let Brian lead her toward the fire. Dylan followed them with his gaze, noting Tad's curious glance from his seat next to Anna.

Madison let out a heavy breath, pulling his attention back to her. "I could have handled her myself." She paused, giving him a sideways glance. "But, thanks."

"Right," Dylan replied, cocking a brow. "Just like you handled her back when she spread all those rumours about us making out in my car at Brent's party?"

Madison snorted a laugh. "I mean, those weren't exactly rumours."

"No, I guess they weren't." His chest warmed at the memory, the first time they'd ever kissed. He had been so nervous, but the look she'd given him that night—

She tucked her hair behind her ear and swept her gaze to his, giving him a shy smile.

He swallowed. *That's the one.*

Marshal's laughter sounded behind them, and Dylan jerked back to reality. He glanced over his shoulder and saw his friend and Sophie returning to the fire, holding hands and giggling like teenagers.

He looked at Madison and nodded toward the house. "How about that non-alcoholic drink?"

"Sophie said Marshal has tea inside. I'm game for something warm." Madison started toward the house, and Dylan fell into step beside her.

Once inside, they kicked off their shoes in Marshal's boot room. Madison flicked on the hallway light and they made their way to the kitchen. Aside from a coffee maker and a fruit basket with a couple of garden squash in it, the woodblock countertops were mostly bare.

"Huh. It's actually clean." Dylan set his cup on the kitchen island. "Last time I was here, it looked a bit more—lived in."

Madison grinned, then shrugged off Dylan's jacket and draped it over one of the chairs. She made her way to the cupboard above the coffee pot. "I'll bet you twenty bucks it's Sophie's doing. His room always looked like a war zone when we were kids."

A copper kettle sat on the counter next to the sink. Dylan filled it with water, set it on the gas-fired range, and turned the heat on to high.

"Thanks." Madison pulled down two ceramic mugs, then eyed the dial on the stove. She glanced at him and turned it a bit to the left.

"Did I do it wrong?" He said with an amused grin. He leaned his hip on the island.

"If it's on high, it could damage the inner lining of the kettle. Medium-high is best." She went back to the cupboard and pulled out a box of Earl Grey. "Earl Grey work for you?"

He gestured at his cup. "I have my cider. But, thanks."

"Suit yourself." She dropped a tea bag into one of the mugs and put the other away, then leaned her back against the counter.

They stood in uncomfortable silence for a few seconds. Dylan's mind reeled, looking for something to say. "So, I hear you're helping out with the inn's harvest festival."

Madison nodded. "I'm organizing the dog shelter fundraiser. How'd you know?"

"Marshal mentioned it," Dylan replied, keeping the part about Marshal warning him to behave around Madison to himself. He frowned. *As if we aren't adults now.* "I'm helping Marshal with his end of things."

"Ah," she replied. "He's putting you to work, is he?"

Dylan bobbed his head. "Yeah. I'll be doing all his manual labour, as usual."

Madison laughed warmly, and his heart hitched. It felt good to make her laugh again.

He continued, "I'm going to the committee meeting tomorrow. If you'd like a ride, I could pick you up."

Her laughter faded, and she tugged at the zipper of her vest. "I don't know if that would be a good idea."

"Why not?"

She bit her lip, regarding him with a serious expression. "Look, if we're going to see each other around, we need to clear the air," she said. "I owe you an apology. Your dad and Ryan—I didn't know. I should have though. I swear, I would have reached out to you if I did."

Dylan's throat thickened, and he rubbed the back of his neck. "I mean, we hadn't talked for years at that point. I didn't expect you to keep tabs on me and my family. And with Jamie—would you even have been able to call me?"

He'd only met the man once at a mutual friend's wedding. It must have been four or five years ago. After Dylan had introduced himself, it was as if a light bulb had gone off in Jamie's head.

Dylan hadn't missed the way the man watched Madison like a hawk and hissed at her through clenched teeth whenever she so much as looked Dylan's way. Other than a quick hello, she didn't even speak to him that night. In fact, she didn't visit with Marshal or Sophie or any of their old friends. She had sat idly beside her husband at their table the whole night, wine glass in hand and a fake smile on her face.

Now, she tilted her head, her chin trembling and a frown on her lips.

A knot formed in Dylan's chest. "I'm sorry. I shouldn't have brought him up."

"No, it's okay. You're right. Two years ago," she paused, "two years ago, I was sleeping on a friend's couch. Jamie had just had a meltdown about my parents, and he'd totally isolated me from them." Her voice grew quiet. "It was the first time he—well, the first time he got physically violent."

Dylan's heart wrenched. Thoughts of tracking down that ratbag and throttling him ran through his mind. He raised his hand. "You don't have to explain."

The kettle began to whistle, and Madison went to the stove and turned it off. She poured hot water into her mug, then carried it to the island and set it down across from him.

"I do," she said, her brown eyes glistening with tears. She took a step around the counter toward him. "Even with everything that happened between us—I mean, I should have been there. I was so wrapped up with everything going on in my own life. I barely spoke to Marshal or Matthew or any of my family at all that year. And when I did, well, things were tense."

The urge to pull her into his arms and hold her, to make her feel safe and ease her pain, rushed through him. *But wouldn't that just make her feel worse? I'm the first schmuck who broke her heart.*

He scrubbed his face with his palm and took a step back. "After what I did to you, you don't owe me a thing."

"Dylan—"

"Look, Madi," he said. "I'm the one who should be apologizing. I took off on you. We had something special, and I ruined it. Dad was sick. We thought we were going to lose him. I couldn't handle it."

He took a deep breath, bad memories pouring through him. "My parents were broke because Dad couldn't work, and I got offered that scholarship. It was a way out. Away from everything."

Madison wiped her cheek, levelling him with her gaze. "Why did you wait until a week before we were supposed to leave? And then you wouldn't answer my calls—"

"I was stupid." Dylan practically spat the word. "I'd gone back and forth for weeks about it, trying to decide what to do. Then I overheard Mom and Dad talking about their money problems, and I couldn't say no. I had to take the scholarship."

"You could have told me."

He winced. "I know. I should have. I was just young and dumb and overwhelmed."

A storm of emotions roiled inside him. What was he supposed to say? *I was in love with you, and it scared me. Instead of turning to you when I needed support, I pushed you away because I was ashamed and terrified of my own feelings?* No, he couldn't add more emotional turmoil to her plate. Not after everything she'd been through.

"Madison, I'm sorry. There's no excuse. But I am really, really sorry."

He reached out and grabbed her hand. To his horror, she flinched and reared backward, a panicked look on her face.

"Oh, no—" he let go of her and held up his hands, the realization of what he'd done slamming into him. "I didn't mean to—" he swallowed. "I'd never hurt you."

She closed her eyes, her hand on her chest. She took a deep breath. "It's okay. I know that. Just, it was a reaction. I guess. I'm not used to—I'm sorry."

The desire to wrap her in his arms to comfort her flamed even higher throughout him. She'd never been skittish before. And now here she was, trembling in fear at the thought of being touched by a man. What had Jamie done to her?

"You have nothing to apologize for," he said, searching for the right words. "We both keep saying sorry. How about we start over?"

A small smile crossed her lips, and her shoulders relaxed. "You're right. Starting over." She paused, her gaze lingering on his. "Hey, Dylan, it's been a while. How are you?"

Dylan forced a grin. "Apparently so full of remorse I might burst. But other than that, I couldn't be better."

He wanted to say more. To tell her that being alone with the most beautiful woman in the world was the reason he couldn't be better. But he bit his tongue, afraid he'd scare her again. Instead, he held out his hand for her to shake.

She tilted her head and placed her hand in his. To his surprise, instead of shaking it, she squeezed his fingers and stepped closer. The smell of citrus mingled with smoke from the campfire wafted over him. She glanced up at him and took a deep breath. "Well, if we're starting fresh, then I think we should free ourselves of all this guilt."

With a lump in his throat, Dylan gently wrapped his arm around her waist. "Is this okay?"

She moved closer, her cheeks turning pink. "Yes. Back there—sudden movements catch me off guard."

He nodded his understanding. With his free hand, he softly brushed a stray lock of hair from her face. "I miss this. I've thought about you for years."

She leaned into his touch, her eyes searching his face. "I thought about you too—"

"I'll be right back!" A feminine voice shouted from Marshal's boot room. The door slammed and footsteps sounded down the hall.

Madison's eyes widened, and she recoiled from Dylan's arms.

He glanced over his shoulder to see Anna standing in the kitchen entrance. She pushed her glasses up her nose, a look of embarrassment on her face. "Oh. Hi. Uh, I didn't realize anybody was in here."

"Hey, Anna." Dylan leaned against the island, trying to look calm. "We were just grabbing Madi some tea."

"Yes. Tea." Madison grabbed her steaming mug and lifted it, her face almost as pink as Anna's. "Earl Grey. Want some?"

Anna glanced between them, then shook her head. "No, I'm okay. Thanks though. I'm just looking for the bathroom."

"Down the hall. Next door on the left," Dylan said.

"Thanks. See you two later."

"See you," Madison replied, her voice a bit too cheery.

Anna left the room. Dylan picked up his cup, the spell broken. He looked at Madison, her cheeks still flushed as she took a sip of her tea.

He swallowed the urge to pull her back into his arms. "Should we head out to the fire?"

"Probably a good idea." Madison used her foot to open the cabinet door beneath the sink, then took the tea bag from her mug and threw it in the garbage. She grabbed Dylan's coat from the chair. "I'm sure Marshal and Sophie will be wondering where we're at. Do you want this back?"

"Nah, you can wear it. You've always suffered in the cold."

Marshal's front door creaked open again and voices floated down the hall.

Definitely time to go.

Dylan led the way to the boot room, nodding hello to several of the other guests he recognized. After pulling on their shoes, they left the house and fell into step beside each other.

As they walked, Madison tucked her hair behind her ear and looked at him from the corner of her eye. "Thanks for that."

"For what?" Dylan asked, his throat dry.

"For clearing the air. I feel better about things. About us."

His pulse quickened with the desire to finish what they had started in Marshal's kitchen. But he couldn't take her hand now, not out here. He couldn't wrap her up and take her home like he wanted to. The only thing he could do was make sure he'd see her again. Soon. *It's now or never, just ask her.*

"If you won't let me pick you up for the committee meeting tomorrow, how about we grab coffee after?"

She narrowed her eyes at him, the corner of her mouth turned up. "Because I still owe you from the other day? After cutting you off with my car?"

Dylan raised a brow, repressing a smile. "No. Because I want to spend more time with you. You don't owe me anything."

They stopped at the fringes of the fire, behind the ring of lawn chairs filled with chatting people. Madison took a sip of her tea, both hands wrapped around the ceramic mug. "All right. Coffee at the inn tomorrow after the meeting."

"It's a date," Dylan replied. *Date?* He held his breath, hoping he hadn't scared her again.

Madison opened her mouth to reply. But before she could speak, Sophie came rushing over from Marshal's side at the food table.

"Madison! There you are." She paused, taking them both in. She tugged on the sleeve of his jacket, still draped on Madison, and cocked her head. "You cold?"

Marshal caught Dylan's eye and beckoned him over.

Here we go. Dylan shoved his free hand in his pocket and gave Madison and Sophie an easy smile. "I'd better go see what Marshal wants. He's waving at me like a nobleman demanding a drink from his butler."

"Always the squire, never the knight," Madison teased with a laugh.

"Ha!" Dylan gave them a wave, then sauntered toward the snack table and Marshal. "We'll see."

Chapter Nine

Thump… thump… thump… Madison cracked one eye open, and a furry tail thwacked against her mattress once more. Before she could block her face, a cold wet nose touched her cheek, followed by loud snuffling noises that could only be from one dog in that house.

"Mack!" She pulled the covers over her face, only to be pummeled by the dog's massive paws on her chest. "Okay, okay. Lay down."

He flopped to the bed and pressed himself up beside her, and she pulled the blanket down to give him a stink eye. His tongue lolled to the side as he gazed at her with adoration, and her heart melted.

"You're too cute to be mad at." She scratched his ears, then blinked at the soft sunshine that shone through the basement window of her room.

What time is it? She sat up, and the movement caused her notebook to slide from her bed to the floor.

Right. Last night. Dylan. Journaling. She glanced at the digital clock on her bookshelf, surprised that it was already ten o'clock. But she hadn't gotten home until after midnight, and then spent over an hour writing out her spinning emotions in that book.

Mack rolled onto his back. She gave his belly a pat, then reached over the bed and picked up the journal from the floor. She hesitated for a moment, then flipped to the last page she'd scribbled on:

I thought Dylan was going to kiss me tonight. I wanted him to.

She swallowed and snapped the journal shut. With a shaking hand, she placed it on her nightstand. It wasn't a lie. She had wanted him to. The memory of him so close, his arm around her waist, gazing at her the way he did when they were teens. As if she were the only woman in the world.

She groaned and flopped onto her back next to Mack. She looked into his amber eyes. "Why, Mack? Why did I have to go into Marshal's kitchen with him? Why did I have to bring up the past?"

His dad. And Ryan. *I had to apologize. I can't believe Marshal didn't tell me.* Her chest felt heavy. It was true, she had been in a terrible place two years ago. But Marshal still should have told her. He could have left her a message.

Could he have, though? Really? It had been the first time she'd actually left Jamie after one of their huge fights. She couldn't even remember what it was about, but she'd never forget the look in his eyes when he backed her into a corner and hit her that first time. She cringed at the memory, her heartrate picking up. She hadn't told anybody. Not even her friend, Carly, whose house she'd stayed at that night.

And when Jamie showed up, I just went home. I took him back, just like that. She balled her fist against her forehead. *What was I thinking? I could have called Dad right then and there. Ended things before they got worse.*

But she hadn't been ready to give up. To face the humiliation that she'd known had been coming for years. She'd married the wrong person. And worse? She'd married an abuser. Somebody who had been abused by his own tyrannical father growing up. Somebody who had sought healing in Madison, giving her a purpose. He'd made her feel important, like she was the only glue that held him together. But soon, the cracks in that glue began to grow until she couldn't hold their marriage—or him—together anymore. And it was her crumbling foundation that took the brunt of his anger.

She took a deep breath and pressed her hands to her eyes to stop the tears from forming. She pictured her counselor, Dr. Theresa, sitting with her legs crossed in her flowy purple dress. The way she tipped her head and gave Madison a sympathetic look and said, "It's not your fault. It wasn't your job to heal him. A marriage is about two people coming together on equal footing, not one person holding the other one together and absorbing all of their pain. That's what punching bags are for, and you my dear, are no human punching bag."

Madison bit her lip, then rolled over to look at Mack. "Two people coming together on equal footing." She paused, her thoughts moving back to Dylan. She huffed. "Equal footing. Yeah right. Dylan Stewart—good job, home to help his mother, beloved by all his friends, apologizes to his awkward ex-girlfriend for freaking out when faced with family tragedy." Her throat thickened. "Madison Talbot—no job, lives at home with her parents, holds a grudge against her ex-boyfriend for a decade, and allowed herself to become a human punching bag."

And I flinched from his touch. Her heart hitched. *More than flinched. I practically recoiled from him in terror. And he*—she squeezed her eyes shut—*he didn't even get upset.*

In fact, he'd softened. Instead of flaring with anger, his eyes had widened with concern. He'd met her moment of fear with the same gentleness he'd always had for her. He'd been sorry for a perfectly normal gesture, that any perfectly normal human in an intimate situation like that would have been comforted by.

She groaned and reached over to stroke Mack's ears. "What am I doing, bud? Going on a date with Dylan? Where could that even go? I'm broken. I can't give him what he deserves."

The faint smell of brewing coffee met her nose, and her dad's voice came from the top of the stairs. "Madison? You up yet?"

Mack lunged from the bed, then bounced in front of the door and let out a whine.

"Yup!" Madison swung her feet to the floor and got up to let Mack out.

He dashed from the room and thundered up the stairs. Madison grabbed her coziest purple cardigan off the top of the chair that sat in the corner of her room and wrapped herself in it. She slipped on her fuzzy slippers and made her way upstairs.

"Morning, Mads. You sure slept in today." Her father sat at the dark walnut table, a steaming coffee cup and his tablet in front of him. His grey hair was still mussed, and he wore a flannel robe and leather slippers. After a busy week at his practice, Saturday mornings were always his time to lounge. He never got out of his pajamas until at least noon, unless they had something special planned.

Mack huffed from his giant bed in the corner of the room, legs splayed out like a newborn foal. Madison went over and scratched his ears, then stretched and followed her nose to the coffee pot on the counter.

"Morning, Dad. Sorry for the late night, hope I didn't wake you and Mom up."

He raised his gaze from the tablet. "We didn't hear a thing. You know your mom, she sleeps like the dead."

"Good thing the dogs do too," Madison replied. She took a mug—the white one with pink hearts and a chip in the handle, her childhood favourite—from the shelf above the coffee maker. After dumping in some cream from the carton on the counter, she filled it with coffee and made her way to the table.

Cupping the mug with both hands and breathing in the delicious aroma, she took the chair across from him. "Caffeine. Just what I need to get the wheels turning."

"Your mom was saying you have that meeting at the inn today," her dad nodded. "Good for you. This could lead to some connections for work. Katie Hoffman would be a great reference." He paused. "You talk to Mrs. Henderson about that bookkeeping job yet?"

"I did, but she said they already filled it."

"Too bad. That would have been a good fit." Bill swiped at his tablet, his attention half on the medical article on the screen. "Keep after her though. They're the only accounting business in town. Surely they'll need more help come year-end. Even a receptionist position—"

"I know, Dad. I'm still looking." Madison tapped the handle of her mug, trying to bury her annoyance. They just wanted what was best for her. But moving home had thrown her back to feeling as if she were seventeen again, and her parents meddling in her affairs wasn't helping.

"All right, kiddo. I know you are." He shot her a comforting smile, the lines crinkling around his bright blue eyes. "So, tell me about Marshal's big to-do last night. Did you have fun? See any old faces?"

Like Dylan Stewart? Madison's face warmed, and she took a comforting sip of coffee. "Yeah. It was great hanging out with Sophie again. Just like old times."

"I'm glad you two have reconnected," Bill said. "She's a great girl. It's about time Marshal saw that."

"Oh, he's seen that for a while," Madison replied. "He was just too scared to do anything about it before."

Her dad chuckled and rubbed his chin. "That may be true. Takes after his old man that way."

Madison grinned. One of her mother's favourite stories was how she and Bill met their first year in college. According to her, the whole year he'd hung around her like a lovesick puppy, going to movies and the mall at her beck and call. *Just like Marshal and Dylan did with me and Sophie.*

She cleared her throat, eyeing her father as he swiped the screen of his tablet again.

"Umm, Dad?" She waited until he looked up. "Why didn't you tell me about Dylan's dad and Ryan?"

His face tightened, and he ran his hand through his hair. Slowly, he said, "Ah. You saw that Stewart boy last night, did you?"

She nodded, trying to force her face to look passive. "Yeah. You guys never told me. Poor Cathy, I can't imagine what they've been going through. I—I should have known."

Her dad set aside the tablet. "I know, Madi-bug. When it happened, you were in such a rough spot. Honestly, we didn't think you needed any more on your plate. Stuff about Dylan always made you—heck,

I didn't even know if you'd answer my phone call."

"You should have tried. Or Marshal should have. Somebody should have."

"I know. I'm sorry." He reached across the table and put his hand on her forearm, his eyes misty. "We did a lot wrong the last few years. Jamie did his best to isolate you from us, and we let him. We should have fought harder, but in the past that didn't go too well."

"I know, Dad." Whirls of anxiety rose in Madison's chest. This wasn't where she'd wanted this conversation to go. She didn't have the energy to deal with this. Not today.

She put her hand on his and squeezed. "I'm sorry too. But what's done is done, and I'm here now. Let's talk about something else." She glanced out the window into the autumn sunshine, then gave him a grave look. "I spotted a new leaf on the lawn yesterday. By the entrance to the lake trail."

Bill took his hand from her arm and leaned back in his chair. "Madison..."

"If you don't get to it soon, it's sure to multiply. You know how those maples are. You should probably pick the tree clean before it sheds everything.

That way, none of those dastardly leaves will ever touch—"

The door to the entry off the kitchen opened, and Mack raised his head and let out a low whoof. Paula entered the room with Dolly at her heels.

"Madison! You're finally up," she teased as she unclipped the poodle's leash. "I thought I was going to have to drag you out of bed by your heels. Don't you have a meeting at the inn today?"

"It's not until one o'clock. I have plenty of time to lounge and eat bonbons all morning."

"If by bonbons you mean the cinnamon buns I picked up yesterday from Forever Cakes, help yourself." Paula gestured to the pantry door.

"Cinnamon buns?" Madison gave her father an aghast look. "Dad, why didn't you tell me?"

He leaned his elbows on the table and shook his head, then took a sip of his coffee.

Madison pushed her chair back from the table and got to her feet. *Who would have thought mom would save me from an uncomfortable conversation? Normally, she's the one forcing them on me.* Her therapist's advice about talking things out with her family rolled in her mind, but she shoved the thought away.

She got to her feet and strode to the pantry, eyeing the familiar yellow box on the back shelf. "There are only two left?"

"We may have got into them last night." Her mother chuckled behind her.

Madison grabbed the box and carried it to the counter, her mouth watering at the smell of cinnamon and cream cheese icing.

Dr. Theresa also said sugar can be an emotional crutch. So really, what does she know?

One hand on the steering wheel, Madison grabbed another Fuzzy Peach from the plastic bag in her console and shoved it in her mouth. The fizzy sweetness practically melted on her tongue, and she bobbed her head happily to the pop song playing on the radio.

Finally, out of that house and away from my parents' nosy questions. She loved them, but their questions about Marshal's party were non-stop. *Did you have a good time? Did you talk to anybody other than Sophie? Did you avoid Dylan like the plague?*

118

Okay, maybe that's not exactly what Mom said. But she had definitely arched her brow when she oh-so-casually asked if he'd been there.

"Yeah. I made out with him in Marshal's hay loft," Madison had replied.

Now, she gave a satisfied laugh at the memory of her mom's red face. She reached for another candy, and her car bounced over a washed-out spot on the gravel road. Suddenly, steam snaked out from beneath her hood and the crimson light of the car's heat gauge flickered on.

What was that? She frowned and turned down the radio. Sure enough, the car sputtered and hissed. The heat gauge began to flash.

"Darn it…"

She guided the car to the side of the gravel road, panic rising in her chest. "This old pile of junk. I should have known better than to buy something off of George's lot!" The man was notorious for buying broken-down vehicles and fixing them himself to sell—the cheapest way possible. Marshal had offered to go with her. But of course, in her rush to get some wheels, she hadn't been willing to wait for him to take an afternoon off work—a decision she was beginning to regret.

She unbuckled her seat belt and got out. *What am I going to do? Look under the hood?* She laughed at the thought, her hands on her hips. She knew absolutely nothing about vehicles. She didn't want to know anything about them.

After taking a deep breath, Madison took her phone from her pocket and glanced at the time. Twelve-thirty. She swallowed a wave of nausea. There was no way she'd make it to the inn by one o'clock. By the time her dad got there and looked her car over or she waited for a tow truck, the meeting would already have started.

Not much else I can do. I'll call Katie after I talk to Dad and let her know. She tapped the screen to pull up her dad's name, ignoring the knot in her stomach.

Chapter Ten

ylan gripped the steering wheel tighter and turned down the gravel road that led to the Starlight Inn. He glanced at the clock as his mom's voice chattered through his speakers. *Fifteen minutes until the meeting. Right on time.*

His mom continued relaying the information she'd gleaned from Christine's card ritual the night before. "She said good things are coming to our family. I drew the Death card!" She paused, as if waiting for him to gasp.

"Okay," Dylan replied. *Not this woo-woo stuff again.* "How is that a good thing? Haven't we had enough death in our lives for a while?"

"It doesn't actually mean somebody's going to die, dear," she replied. "It means change. And combined with the Sun card, it could mean big changes! I'm a beginner at this, Christine can explain it better."

"Great." Dylan sighed, trying to humour her. "But I'm trying to avoid change. I want to stay in Cedar Lake."

"Have you heard back from Jason yet?"

"No news yet, Mom," he said. "But I'm trying."

"Have you thought more about consulting? I think you'd do well at it. You have the connections."

"I don't know, Mom. Sun Tech has been good to me. Let's see what Jason says first."

The truth was, he *had* considered starting his own consulting business. But it would mean a lot of work and a big pay cut, at least at first. With his mom all alone and his plans to start Natalie a college fund—it just didn't seem feasible. Not right now.

Besides, Jason hasn't given me a firm answer yet, he reminded himself. If things went his way, he could stay with Sun Tech, live in Cedar Lake, and keep that paycheque. He just had to be patient and let Jason work things out. Maybe by summer he could put his condo in Vancouver up for sale.

Maybe he could start hunting for a proper home in Cedar Lake. A nice bungalow, something he could settle down in with somebody special—

Don't get ahead of yourself.

"Well, let me know what he says," his mom replied. "And keep thinking of other options. Christine says you should think outside the box, and I agree."

"Christine says a lot of things," Dylan replied. "Look Mom, I better go. I'm almost at the inn."

"Okay, dear. I'll talk to you later. Don't forget to grab something for Natalie's birthday on Friday." She paused. "You know, you could invite somebody—"

"Bye, Mom."

"Just give it some thought. Goodbye, dear."

Dylan pressed the button on his steering wheel to end the call, a wave of relief rolling through him. He knew exactly who his mom had in mind for him to invite, and he wasn't sure how he felt about it. Obviously, inviting Madison to his niece's birthday party was out of the question. It was far too soon. He wasn't even sure if they were friends again.

But they were at least on better footing. Since last night, he hadn't been able to get the thought of her lovely smile out of his mind. The memory of the way she leaned into his touch, even after he'd bone-headedly grabbed her hand as if they were together.

She must feel it too, right? Despite everything they'd gone through over the years, both together and apart, she'd been willing to see him again. What they had before had been so special, he'd never found anything like it since. None of the other women he'd dated had captured him the way Madison did.

Don't we owe it to ourselves to explore this? If we take things slow—

His Explorer rumbled over a washed-out section of gravel, jerking his attention back to the road. A familiar rusted blue car sat on the shoulder ahead of him, a woman in a burgundy peacoat standing beside it. *Madison?*

He slowed his truck and pulled up behind her, a hint of humour rolling through him. She glanced at him and he gave her a quick wave, then opened his door and got out.

"Hey, Mads. You need that ride to the meeting after all?"

Her face red, she jerked her hand in the direction of the steaming hood. "Look at this heap of garbage! I called my dad. He's on his way to look at it, but he's no better with engines than I am. He's a doctor, not a mechanic."

"What happened?"

"I don't know. It's junk. I knew it was junk when I bought it. But it's all I could afford." She frowned. "Dad said he'd drive me to the inn for the meeting and come back to wait for the tow truck. But I don't know if I'll make it." She glanced at her phone. "It starts in about ten minutes."

"Why don't you shoot him a text and hop in with me?" Dylan asked. "I can bring you back here after."

"What about our coffee?"

He shoved his hands in his pockets, trying to hide his disappointment. "We can do it another day. Or, if you don't mind, we can still have coffee and I'll bring you home after."

She tapped her chin, and he could practically see the wheels turning in her head.

He jerked his head toward his SUV. "Sound like a plan?"

"It's just, my parents." She tucked a strand of hair behind her ear and gave him an embarrassed look. "I don't know what they'd think if you came rolling in the drive with me in your passenger seat."

He raised his brows. "Ah. I take it I'm not their favourite person. Since, you know—"

"It's not that," she said, the colour creeping from her cheeks to her ears. "Well, maybe it is." She paused. "You know what? I'm twenty-eight years old." She swiped at her phone and tapped frantically on the screen. "I'm not seventeen. If I want to have coffee with you, I can. I can date whoever I darn well please."

Date? He couldn't hide his smile.

She looked up at him. "What?"

"Nothing," Dylan replied. "Just wondering what type of girl goes on a date with the squire instead of the knight?"

"If my memory is correct, the knight's my brother," Madison shot back. "So the squire will have to do." She jammed her phone in her pocket. "Besides, who said it was a date?"

He gave her a sideways look. "You did."

She opened her mouth, as if ready to fire back a sassy retort. But instead, she gave him an embarrassed smile. "I guess I did. In that case, are you ready to escort me to the royal inn?"

Dylan chuckled. "If by *royal* you mean *backwoods*, you got it." He made his way to the passenger side of his vehicle and opened the door for her.

She gave her car one last glare, then walked to the Explorer and climbed inside.

After getting in and buckling his seat belt, Dylan put the SUV in drive and started down the road toward the inn. He flicked on the passenger seat warmer.

After a few seconds, Madison let out a dreamy sigh and ran her hand over the leather seat. "This is nice, thank you."

"Not a problem." Dylan glanced at her from the corner of his eye. She looked perfect there, riding next to him in his Explorer. As if she belonged. And the way she'd curled her hair—did she do it for him? Or was she trying to impress the Hoffmans? He tore his gaze from her and looked at the clock on the dash.

"We might be a couple minutes late, but I doubt they'll start on time anyways."

"Do they usually have issues with people coming late?" Madison asked.

Dylan shrugged. "More like Katie and Rodger are pulled in twenty different directions all the time. They could really use some more help around there. Sophie steps in a lot, but she's pretty busy in the kitchen."

"Well, good thing they have volunteers like us. Hopefully we can get the festival off the ground smoothly."

They were quiet for a moment, Madison leaning into the warm seat with her hands clasped on her lap. She opened her mouth, as if about to speak, but then pressed her lips together.

Dylan caught her eye. "Everything okay?"

"Yes," she replied slowly, fiddling with the sleeve of her jacket. "I guess I just wanted to thank you."

"For what? Driving you to the inn?" Dylan shrugged. "I'm heading there anyways."

"No," she replied softly. "For the other night. For not freaking out when I flinched away from you."

"Why would I freak out over that?" *What the heck did that scumbag do to her?*

"I don't know. Some people would." She darted her gaze out the window. "It was just really nice to be, you know, treated gently. With understanding. So, thank you."

Dylan wasn't sure what to say. He'd been horrified that he'd scared her to begin with. But now she was thanking him for being kind?

He licked his lips and gave her a serious look. "I hope you know you should be treated like that all the time. Whatever he did to you, that's not normal. You didn't deserve it. Any of it. That's on him."

"Dylan, I wasn't perfect either—"

"It doesn't matter. Whatever he did, it wasn't okay." He swallowed the burning sensation in his throat. "Nobody deserves to be abused, but especially you. You—" *Are what? Are the most perfect woman on the planet? And I was an idiot to push you away?* "You are kind. You are passionate. You are hardworking and loyal. You are one of the best people I know." He paused. "Even when you're being sassy."

Her tight face melted into a smile, her eyes misty. "You've barely even seen me for ten years. I've changed."

"We both have," he replied. "But in the midst of your whole life upheaving, you're volunteering for a dog shelter and helping the Hoffmans with this festival. That's pretty amazing. And besides, you haven't changed that much. You can still dish it out and put me in my place when I need it."

Madison let out a soft laugh, then reached across the console and laced her fingers through his. "Thanks. I'm glad we're having coffee today."

At her touch, the tension eased from his chest. He gently stroked the back of her hand with his thumb. "Me too."

She was safe now, away from that monster. And whether they ended up together or not, Dylan would never hurt her. He wouldn't blow it this time. He'd make up for his past mistakes.

They approached a large white sign for the Starlight Inn. He let go of her hand and turned the Ford down the gravel driveway, enjoying the scenic views of the horses at pasture with the vibrant fall colours surrounding them.

Several cars were parked in front of the main building, and he spotted Marshal standing on the front deck with his farm hand, Beena Kumar.

He let go of Madison's hand and pulled into the parking spot next to his friend's market truck. They got out of the Explorer and made their way up the creaky wooden steps to the front porch.

Marshal met them by the door with Beena behind him. "Hey, guys. I didn't know you were coming together."

"My car broke down," Madison replied shortly. "Dylan was driving by, so he stopped and gave me a ride." She glanced at Beena. "Hey, Beena."

Beena smiled at her from beneath the brim of her ball cap, her long black hair tied behind her head in a braid. "Hi, Madison. Good to see you again."

Marshal crossed his arms and cast Dylan a curious look. "Isn't that convenient."

"You know me," Dylan shrugged, "always saving the day. Picking up people stuck on the side of the road or hunting down pumpkins, I'm on it."

Marshal snorted. "I figured that car wouldn't last long."

Madison whirled on him, her cheeks turning red. "Don't start—"

Her brother held up his hands. "I'm not. Did you call Dad?"

"He's on his way to meet the tow truck. Geez, Marsh." Madison grabbed the front door handle and yanked it open. "Stop hovering. I'm not a helpless child."

Without looking back, she stomped inside.

Marshal huffed. "Who peed in her corn flakes?"

"She's got a point," Beena replied.

Dylan chuckled at Marshal's scowl, then followed Madison inside.

Dylan poured black coffee into his mug and returned the pot to the burner, his gaze on Madison's back. She leaned against the island across from him in the inn's cozy kitchen, chatting animatedly with Anna.

The festival meeting had ended a few minutes ago, and Anna had pulled Madison aside to discuss volunteering at Pawsitive Match. As welcoming as always, Sophie had greeted them in the kitchen and told them to make themselves at home.

Now, Sophie sauntered up beside him, a carton of cream in her hand. "Did you grab yourself a cup?"

He raised his mug and nodded, breathing in the rich aroma. "You bet. This from Valley Roast?"

"Of course. We're all about supporting local business." She reached around him and picked up the ceramic pitcher from the tray next to the coffeemaker and began to fill it with the cream. "That was nice of you to pick up Madison for the meeting."

Dylan shifted aside to give her more room. "I mean, she broke down on the side of the road. It would have been pretty heartless to just drive on by."

Sophie set the now-full pitcher back in its spot. "Well, aren't you the biggest gentleman lately?"

"Aren't I always?"

She tossed the empty cream carton in the recycling box beneath the counter, then turned to him. "You know what I mean." She counted on her fingers. "Buying Madison coffee, taking her into Marshal's house for tea, giving her a lift to the meeting," she paused, "lending her your jacket..."

Dylan took another sip of his coffee.

What's with the inquisition? Sure, he and Madison hadn't ended their teenaged relationship on a good note. But that was years ago. Things were different now. Did Sophie and Marshal really think he and Madison hadn't grown at all? That they were bound for the same mistakes all over again?

He cleared this throat. "You and Marshal sure seem interested in our interactions."

"Oh, Dylan. Do you think it's a good idea for you two to," she waved her hand in front of her, "you know? Start something."

"I'm not out to hurt her, Soph."

Sophie bit her lip, following his gaze to Madison and Anna. "She's just been through so much."

"Madison isn't some fragile chick that needs you and Marshal flapping around," he swallowed the tightness in his throat, then lowered his voice. "She's the strongest woman I know. She had the gumption to leave that goon of an ex-husband, do you really think she can't handle spending time with me?" He paused. "Am I so horrible?"

"I didn't mean it like that. You know Marshal and I both adore you. You're practically a brother to him."

Sophie clasped her hands in front of her. "But, there are old feelings between you and Madi that are hard to forget. And besides, aren't you moving back to Vancouver soon?"

"Things might change. I'm talking with my boss about staying here permanently." Dylan set his mug on the counter, his gaze still lingering on Madison's back. "Look, Madison can make up her own mind. And don't you think you should bring this up with her, not me?"

As if on cue, Madison tossed back her head with a laugh at something Anna said. Her chocolate brown curls cascaded down her back, and Dylan's neck grew warm.

He looked at Sophie. "Sure, we have a history. But in case you've forgotten, there was a lot more good than bad. I'd do anything to make it up to her, even if we just end up as friends and nothing more."

Sophie's face softened. "Okay. I'll back off. I know your heart's in the right place. Just be careful. I know she's strong, but her soul's still mending."

At the mention of *soul*, Christine's frizzy hair and tarot cards popped into Dylan's mind. He raised a brow.

"Now I see it."

Sophie tilted her head. "See what?"

"Your mom. I never saw much of her in you before." He picked up his mug and took a satisfying drink. "But you just gave me a glimpse."

Sophie wrinkled her nose, then let out a laugh. "Oh, please."

Before she could go any further, the French doors swung open and Katie Hoffman strode into the room, her heels clacking on the tiled floor.

Katie stopped next to Sophie and tucked her clipboard beneath her arm, her face tired. "Let's put a fresh pot of coffee on. I need at least three cups." She glanced at Dylan. "Hey, Dylan. Thanks for coming out today and volunteering to help with the festival."

"No problem." He shoved his free hand in his pocket. "I've got Friday off, so I can come set up the pumpkin patch with Marshal and anything else you might need."

"You have no idea how much we appreciate that," she replied. "It's one thing after another with this festival. One week away and everything's falling apart."

Sophie poured the last of the coffee into a mug and handed it to her. "What's going on now?"

Katie set her clipboard on the counter, then took the coffee from her with a grateful groan. "Thank you. Pure caffeine. I think I need an IV filled with it." She blew on her steaming cup and took a sip. "You know those square hay bales we're supposed to pick up from the Johnsons' farm?"

Sophie nodded. "Yeah, Rodger and Tad were heading out right after the meeting to go load them."

Katie shook her head, cradling her mug with both hands. "Not anymore. Dane just came running from the barn, faster than I've ever seen him move. Apparently, Old Joe and Henry got out. The back fence was wide open."

Sophie covered her mouth. "Did Ethan forget to latch the chain again? Dane's going to kill him!"

"Old Joe?" Dylan asked. "Why does it sound like your elderly neighbours have escaped?"

"Two of our Clydesdales," Katie said with a sigh. "Old Joe is notorious for getting out. He's learned to flip the latch on the gate. And Henry, his partner in crime, follows along for the ride. Luckily, their corral borders the neighbour's farm.

But they're out on fifty wooded acres and aren't easy to catch."

Sophie pushed a stray copper strand of hair from her face. "So Rodger and Tad had to take the truck and horse trailer over to the Pattersons' to haul them home?"

"Yes. And we don't have anything else to pull the trailer for the bales."

Dylan finished his coffee and set the mug on the counter. "That little flat-deck? My Explorer could handle it. It has a hitch I've used to haul my mom's camper."

"Really?" Katie asked with a relieved expression. "I would appreciate it more than you know. The Johnsons want the bales out of their shed before tomorrow to make room for more, and I'd hate for them to get rained on before the festival."

Sophie snapped her gaze to his. "Don't you have plans with Madison?"

Madison looked over her shoulder. "Did I hear my name?" She flipped her hair behind her back and made her way over to them.

Dylan gestured to Katie. "Katie needs somebody to pick up some bales for the festival. Want to have our coffee on the road?"

"Sure." Madison eyed the coffeemaker. "But we better make another pot. I'm running low on fuel."

"Perfect!" Katie finished her coffee and set her empty cup next to Dylan's. "Follow me, I'll show you where the trailer is and help you hook up. Thanks again. You're saving us a huge headache."

"It's no problem," Dylan replied. "I'm always up for a drive through the countryside."

"And manually loading fifty bales onto a trailer?" Katie arched a brow.

"You bet." He glanced at Madison, who was smiling warmly at something Sophie said. *I'm up for doing anything with her by my side.*

CHAPTER ELEVEN

Madison leaned back in the passenger seat, enjoying the warmth that seeped through the canvas jacket she'd borrowed from Dylan. They drove down the highway in the late afternoon sun with fifty square bales loaded securely on the trailer.

They sat in amiable silence, Dylan watching the road and Madison's eyes drooping with exhaustion. Despite her aching muscles, contentment filled her. Sure, loading hay bales wasn't exactly the intimate afternoon of catching up with Dylan that she'd envisioned. But the physical labour had felt good. And their easy banter—she hadn't laughed and felt at such ease with a man for a long time.

Even when Dylan slipped and dropped one of the bales, his good nature shone through. The twine had broken, causing the bale to fall apart. She'd held her breath, halfway expecting him to start raging the way Jamie would have. But Dylan had just given her that goofy smile, shrugging in self-defeat. Together, they'd cleaned up the loose flakes and tied the bale back together as best they could. It looked a bit disfigured, but Dylan had assured her that it would be fine for feeding the horses.

Now, Madison clenched her fists and rubbed them against the rough fabric of her coat. *Jamie would have flipped.* They'd never had a project go smoothly. Her stomach twisted as she remembered when they'd put Mack's kennel together. Jamie had thrown the kennel door across the room, his face beet red. The door had gouged the wall, but that was nothing compared to the holes he'd punched in it in previous fits of rage. Kicking tool boxes, snapping boards, yelling at her for every tiny misstep—that behaviour had become a common occurrence in their apartment. Normal, even.

She glanced at Dylan, who watched the road with a slight smile on his roughly shaven face.

She'd known him since elementary school, and the only time she'd heard him raise his voice at anyone was in grade seven in Marshal's defense. A bully had been teasing her brother for being that weird boy who liked to garden. Even then, Dylan hadn't lashed out, managing to turn the tables on the bully and send him away without coming to blows. He and Marshal had been best friends ever since.

And that afternoon, he'd been so, well, mature. He'd let her arrange the bales on the trailer however she saw fit. The only hand he'd raised had been placed on her waist to steady her when she climbed on the stack to adjust the tie-down strap. It had all been so natural—and so refreshingly respectful. She'd almost forgotten what it felt like to be treated like that.

With one hand on the wheel, Dylan grabbed his travel mug from the cupholder between them and gave it a swirl. He frowned. "Nothing left. Too bad we have the trailer, or I'd whip into Valley Roast."

"I'm sure Sophie will be happy to put coffee on when we get back," Madison replied. She twisted to reach the backseat and into the pocket of her peacoat, then pulled out the half-full bag of Fuzzy Peaches.

"In the meantime, I have candy to hold us over." She shook the baggy. "Want one?"

"Sure." He set his travel mug back in the cupholder and held out his hand.

She gave him a couple of candies, then popped one in her mouth, closing her eyes. "Mmm. Sugar. Life's greatest gift."

"After coffee, of course," Dylan replied, chewing slowly. "Hey, do you mind if we take a little detour?"

Madison sat straighter, peering through the windshield. "Detour? Where are we gonna go with all these bales?"

"Trust me, I think you'll like it."

She gave him a sideways look, but nodded, curious about what he had in mind. "Okay. Let's see what you have up your sleeve."

The area they were in was filled with horse paddocks, U-pick berry farms, and orchards—all closed for the season. Everything except for the lake.

Her heart hitched. *The lake!*

She could hardly contain her excitement as they rolled up to the green road sign. A white arrow pointed toward a dirt parking lot with a gate leading to a familiar trail. *Cedar Lake.*

Dylan turned into the drive. "The gates are still open. Want to walk down to the beach?"

"Yes!" Without thinking, Madison reached across the console and squeezed his forearm, emotion stirring inside her. When they were teens, they'd spent so much time at the lake, her dad had started calling her *Ogopogo*. Swimming, kayaking with Marshal and Sophie, tenting beneath the cedar trees, huddling around a campfire laughing and telling stories, reading romance books in the sun. It almost felt like home.

Dylan parked along the edge of the empty parking lot, leaving plenty of room for the trailer. Madison pinched the bag of candy closed and shoved it in her pocket, unbuckled her seatbelt, and scrambled from the vehicle.

Dylan joined her and they made their way onto the path toward the lake. Her heart thrumming inside her, she slipped her hand into his. He intertwined their fingers, and her anxiety calmed. *This feels so natural, being here with him.*

She squeezed his hand. "Remember that one Canada Day when we were camping here, and Sophie made us that huge bowl of Greek salad?"

Dylan wrinkled his nose. "You mean when she was so proud of finding fresh olives at the farmer's market, and didn't realize you had to cure them first?"

"And Marshal sat there sneakily picking them off his plate so she wouldn't see, thinking he was the only one who didn't like them." Madison chuckled.

"He's a good man," Dylan replied.

"You didn't hide your disgust for one second." She nudged him playfully.

"I couldn't help but wonder if she was trying to kill us."

They hit the end of the path, where the trees receded and a beach sprawled out in front of them. The sun, now dipping behind the mountain on the other side of the lake, cast an orange glow across the valley. A familiar dock stretched out onto the still water, faded with years of wear.

They were quiet for a moment, Madison reveling in the beautiful evening. She edged closer to Dylan's side, and he put his arm around her. Her chest warmed at his touch. It felt as if nothing had happened between them. No emotional teenage break-up, no decade apart.

No, something has changed. Their dynamic had shifted. The old spark and comfort were there, but the awkwardness and unsureness of youth had disappeared. He stood next to her as a man. A good man, with no hint of anger threatening to strike out at a moment's notice.

She tilted her head to glance up at him, noting the lines on his face as he gazed at the water.

"Dylan?"

He looked down at her. "What's up?"

"This is nice. Like, really nice." She bit her lip, unsure of what to say. "And I had such a great day with you—" *Just tell him. Pull up your big girl pants, Madison. For once.* "Are we starting something here?"

His lips twitched with a smile, his voice husky. "Do you want to start something?"

Her heart in her throat, she nodded.

Dylan let out a breath, his eyes searching her face. He lowered his lips to hers, and she met him softly, melting into the kiss.

A siren noise blared from Dylan's jacket, jerking them from the moment. He startled, then pulled his phone from his pocket and pressed the button on the side to silence it.

"I'm sorry!" He scowled at the device. "I should have put this thing on vibrate. The siren—it's for my boss." He gave her a weak smile. "Like, emergency. Because it never is." He paused. "It's a joke. It's dumb, I know."

The phone flashed in his hand, and Madison began to laugh. "Take it. I'll be right here."

Dylan hesitated, rubbing the back of his neck. "You sure?"

"Totally." She waved her hands in his direction, as if to hurry him along. "I promise, I won't take off."

"Good. Uh—thanks." He tipped his head to her, then stepped away with a sheepish grin and took the call.

Still lightheaded from their kiss, she grabbed her phone from her pocket to distract herself. She'd left it in the Ford that afternoon while they loaded bales and hadn't checked it since. She turned on the screen and cringed at the six missed calls—all from two numbers she didn't recognize.

That's weird.

As she pulled up her voicemail, Dylan's voice floated over her.

"I don't want to start the new year by going back to Vancouver. Did you show him my daily updates? This is working."

Vancouver? Madison frowned. *What's he talking about? He didn't mention—*

The monotone voice from her mailbox informed her that it was full. Staring at Dylan's back, she hit the number one on the keypad to listen to the first message.

A slew of profanity met her ear, and her heart stopped. Jamie's angry voice hurled obscenities at her. She gasped and dropped the phone, her throat constricting. She gaped in horror at the device on the ground, muffled expletives still spewing from the speaker.

"Madison?" Dylan was suddenly at her side. "You okay?"

"Uh—" she flicked her gaze to his, her mind blank. "I don't know."

Dylan looked at the phone, then back to her. "Was that who I think it was?"

Madison's knees buckled, her stomach in knots. She nodded.

He gently slipped his arm around her side. She twisted and leaned into his chest, fighting the bile that rose in her throat.

"I'm so sorry." He wrapped both arms around her, holding her tight. "You're safe now. He can't get to you."

Her mind whirled, the numbness broken. *Yes, he can! He knows where I live. He knows where my parents live. He—*

Dylan stroked her hair, repeating himself in a gentle voice. "You're safe, Madi. You're safe."

She squeezed her eyes shut and focused on his soothing words. She allowed his warmth to envelop her, willing her heartrate to slow.

Dylan looked down at her, his face creased with concern. "Are you okay?"

She swallowed, her body still weak. "Can we just stand here a minute? Stay like this?"

"Of course," he murmured, stroking her hair once more. "As long as it takes."

Madison pressed her cheek against his chest and let a tear fall, the panic in her chest easing away.

Chapter Twelve

Madison yawned into her elbow, holding the paring knife away from her. She stood at the island in her mother's kitchen, the late-afternoon sunshine warming her back through the window. A cutting board with a half-sliced apple lay before her, and a salad bowl filled with spinach and various other ingredients sat next to it.

Sophie stood across from her, whisking oil and mustard together for the dressing. They were preparing Sophie's famous autumn apple salad, a favourite of guests at the inn, for the Talbot family's Sunday dinner.

Madison finished cutting the apple and tossed the slices on the spinach. "You said just one apple, right?"

Sophie spooned some honey into the dressing mixture. "That should be right. I usually make much larger batches of this for the inn, but I calculated the ingredients per person." She paused, eyeing the bowl. "Do you think your family would like more fruit in it? I brought more cranberries."

"I'm sure it's fine," Madison replied. "Between all the fruit and honey, there should be enough sweetness to get my dad to eat it."

Sophie laughed. "Marshal said he's a meat-and-potatoes kind of guy." She gave the dressing one final whisk, then set the bowl aside.

"He'll graciously try the salad. Alongside a heaping mountain of Mom's shepherd's pie." Madison glanced at the timer on the stove. They'd popped in a frozen dish her mom had made up after Thanksgiving a few weeks ago with the leftover mashed potatoes. It was an old family recipe, and her father's favourite.

Just what he needs after our stressful morning at the police station.

Sophie leaned her hip against the island, looking at Madison. "Are you doing okay? You know, after everything that happened these last twenty-four hours. It's been intense."

"I'm fine," Madison replied with a shrug. "I mean, I'm exhausted. After talking things through with Dylan and unloading bales, I didn't get home until late. And then explaining Jamie's voicemail to Mom and Dad this morning, and going to the police station to make a report—" She shuddered. "I mean, it went okay. But I'm glad it's over. "

Sophie gave her a sympathetic look. "I don't know how you did it. You are one brave lady."

Brave? More like struggling to climb out of a thousand-foot hole I dug myself to begin with.

"It's not like I had a choice." Madison picked up the dirty cutting board and placed it in the sink, then grabbed a dishrag to wipe down the island. "You should have seen me when I heard the voicemail. Complete breakdown. Thank goodness I wasn't alone."

Sophie put the lids on the salad bowl and the dressing. "That's right. Dylan." She gave Madison a sly look. "How did he handle that?"

Madison set the cloth on the counter and crossed her arms. "Sophie Walsh, are you digging for gossip? If I didn't know any better, I'd think you were hanging around with Ashley Adams."

"Umm, no." Sophie snorted. "I'm not hanging out with Ashley. I'm just curious. Can't a girl be concerned about her best friend?"

"I didn't think you two would be buddies," Madison replied. "But she was at Marshal's party—"

"Oh, stop." Sophie waved her off. "So, things went okay today with the police?" She picked up the salad bowl, carried it to the fridge, and placed it inside. She returned to the island for the dressing. "And with Dylan?"

"Yes, things went fine." Madison's cheeks grew warm, thinking of the previous night with him. How he'd held her on the beach, whispering calming words in her ear, helping her find her bearings before the panic in her head completely swept her away.

And before that, their kiss.

"You're blushing!" Sophie gave her a cat-like grin. "You never blush. Come on."

"Okay." Madison glanced out the window above the sink. Her dad and Marshal were out at the shed, looking over her dad's garden tractor. "But please don't tell Marshal anything. Not yet.

He's weird about Dylan."

"He's just worried," Sophie replied. "But yes, I promise my lips are sealed until you're ready."

"Dylan and I," Madison swallowed, "well, he kissed me."

"He did?" Sophie let out a muffled squeal, her eyes wide. "Madison! Why didn't you tell me?"

"Because!" Madison lowered her voice, butterflies forming in her stomach. "We're taking it slow. Nothing's official."

"Hmm." Sophie hugged her elbows, as if barely able to contain herself. "I mean, it's exciting. I think he's grown up a lot. But how are you feeling about it? Do you think it's a good idea?"

Madison pressed her lips together. The truth was, she wasn't sure if it was a good idea or not. But it felt right. When she'd heard Jamie's furious voice through that speaker, it had hit her like a freight train. Every angry fit, seething conversation, physical blow—it had all come rushing back to her. She'd lost control of her life again in that split second, at the whim of an angry bull determined to tear her down.

But then Dylan had wrapped her in his comforting arms. The way his warmth enveloped her like a fortress against the outside world, making her feel safe and grounded. She'd never had anything like that before. Not even with him, when they'd dated before. And certainly not with Jamie.

She moved her gaze to Sophie. "I can't explain it, Soph. It was as if he knew exactly what to do last night to calm me down. Do you know how big of a deal that is? I haven't felt safe with a guy for a long time. My danger radar is constantly on high alert. But with Dylan, I can relax. Having him with me, I could face anything." She paused, running her hand through her loose waves. "Ugh. Why am I being so cheesy? Seriously, snap me out of it."

Sophie gave her a misty look, then wiped beneath her eye.

"Are you crying?"

"No!" Sophie sniffed. "It's just, I was worried about you two seeing each other. And I'm sorry if this annoys you, but I even tried to feel him out about it at the festival meeting."

"You talked to him?" Madison shook her head, but she couldn't be angry. Sophie had always had the best intentions. Even when they were fifteen years old and Madison caught her passing notes to Dylan asking if he thought Madison was cute.

Sophie reached across the island and grasped Madison's hand. "But it feels right, doesn't it? Like our lives are aligning, right where they should be."

"Soph, you're starting to sound like your Mom and all her spiritual psychobabble," Madison teased. She took a deep breath, pushing her emotions aside. "We're just two people figuring things out. Besides, he might have to move back to Vancouver."

Her heart sank at the thought. After her meltdown, Dylan had told her what was going on with his job. He assured her that he was trying his best to stay in Cedar Lake, but they'd both agreed to take things slow until they knew where their futures lay.

Heck, Madison had no idea if she'd permanently live in Cedar Lake either. If she didn't find a job soon…

"Vancouver's not that far." Sophie squeezed her fingers, then let go. "Besides—"

The back door swung open, and Marshal stepped inside with her father behind him.

"Hey, ladies." He hesitated, taking in their serious gazes and what Madison was sure were red-nosed, watery-eyed faces. "What's going on?"

"We're just getting supper ready," Sophie replied. She picked up the dressing and carried it to the fridge. "Autumn apple salad. You said you liked it last time we ate at the inn."

Madison's dad kicked off his boots, then sniffed the air. "Something smells good! Is that shepherd's pie?"

"Mom's famous recipe." Madison cringed at the fake-cheer in her voice. "You guys wash up. Mom should be back from her walk with the dogs soon."

Marshal caught her eye for a moment, then ducked into the half-bath next to the entrance.

No more talk about Dylan or Jamie or everything complicated in my life. Madison stepped to the farmhouse sink and turned on the tap. She gazed at the vibrant orange and red foliage at the edge of the lawn, and her shoulders relaxed.

A family supper would be just what she needed— some sort of normalcy in her life. Having Sophie there, now part of her family, made it all the better. Before she could catch herself, her mind wandered to thoughts of Dylan pulling in the drive and joining them.

She took a breath and turned off the tap. *One day at a time, Madison. You don't even know if things with him are real yet.*

After dinner, Madison sat outside at the patio table on the porch, wrapped in her knit wool sweater. The sun had just disappeared below the trees, taking its warm rays with it. Even though mosquito season had passed, she'd still lit the citronella candle in the middle of the synthetic table. Its flame cast a comforting glow over her.

Mack, who lay at her feet, let out a satisfied yawn. She stroked his ears, happy for the quiet peace.

"Well," she said to him, "that wasn't quite the relaxing meal I'd hoped for."

Nothing big had happened, but her parents had been tense. Her mother had watched Madison like a hawk over the rim of her wine glass. And while her father had avoided the topic of the police and what had gone on that day, Paula hadn't been afraid to pepper her with questions.

After taking a particularly large drink, she'd shot Madison a pointed look. "Have you heard back from the police yet?"

"No, Mom. It's only been a few hours."

Paula had given Bill an anxious glance. "Maybe you should call the Vancouver department. Who knows if Constable Hawking has even contacted them yet?"

"Let the man do his job," Bill had replied. "He'll get it looked after."

"And what if this slips through the cracks? That jerk will just keep bothering Madi—"

"I blocked his number, Mom. It's fine," Madison had said, her face hot.

"It's not fine."

At this point, Marshal had looked up from his meal and interjected. "Mom, could we just have a nice supper and talk about this later? Madi said she's okay. It's dealt with."

Madison hadn't been that grateful for him in a long time. Not since they were kids, and he'd taken the blame when she destroyed her mom's petunia bed with her out-of-control bike. She reminded herself to thank him later.

The sound of the door opening brought her attention back to the present. Marshal appeared, wearing his flannel jacket, with two steaming mugs in his hands. He set them on the table, then took the seat across from her.

He nodded his head at the cups. "Peppermint tea. Sophie thought you'd like some."

"Thanks. How much sugar did she put in it?"

"Probably none." Marshal grimaced. He reached down and patted Mack's head. "Hey, bud."

Madison picked up the mug, grateful for its warmth. "Hey, thanks for stepping in back there. Derailing another one of Mom's rants. I owe you one."

Marshal shrugged and leaned back in his chair. "She's just worried about you, Mads. She's scared Jamie is going to show up out here. Not to scare you, but it happens."

"Oh, I know." Madison took a sip of her tea, letting the warm mint soothe her throat. "But I'm being careful. I blocked his number, and the cops are on top of things.

Constable Hawking said the Vancouver police department would be looking into it.”

“What’s going to happen to him?”

“It sounded like breaking the restraining order will be added to his charges,” Madison replied. “He’ll probably only get a fine, though. It would be different if he confronted me in person.”

Marshal grunted and rubbed his temple. “They should throw him in jail.”

“I wish they could. But at least this has been added to his record.”

“Better than nothing, I guess.” Marshal leaned forward and gave her a serious look. “But you be careful, okay?”

“I’m not a princess in need of saving.”

He held up his hand. “I’m serious, Madison. Guys like Jamie—”

“I know what he’s like, Marsh.” She held his gaze. “Better than most. He was drunk and being stupid. I doubt he’d come out here. Something set him off, probably something his lawyer told him. But I’m okay.” She nodded firmly, but she wasn’t sure if she meant to comfort her brother or herself.

They were quiet for a moment, then Madison set her tea on the table. "Besides, I'm surrounded by support. He's not gonna get through you, or Mom and Dad, or even Sophie."

Marshal tapped his fingers on the table. "Or Dylan?"

She froze. *He's going to start in on that?*

"I saw the way you two were looking at each other the other night," he said. "And at the festival meeting. And him picking you up, spending last night together—"

Madison narrowed her eyes at him. "You're sure keeping tabs on me, huh? Besides, in case you forgot, my car broke down. It's not even here, Dad had it towed to Barry's shop yesterday. I needed a ride."

"Look, I'm not trying to be nosy."

"But you are being nosy, Marshal David Talbot." Annoyance flickered in Madison's chest. "What's it to you, anyway? Dylan's your best friend. It's not like you hate the guy."

"Of course I don't hate him." Marshal let out a huff. "But come on, there's rocky history between you two. And you're hurting already. I'm just worried—"

Madison slapped the edge of the table. "Oh, for crying out loud! Everybody's worried about me.

All the time. It's exhausting."

Marshal opened his mouth to say something, but she cut him off. "I appreciate the support. You know that. But give me some credit." She took a deep breath and lowered her voice. "Yes, this weekend I reconnected with Dylan. But it's not like we're jumping into anything. And you know what? It was just by chance he was there when I got that voicemail from Jamie. But he handled it pretty darn well. Better than our parents, that's for sure."

Marshal's face softened, and he ran his hand through his hair. "Okay. I get it."

"And don't get any ideas about talking to him about it, either." Madison fixed him a piercing look. "I mean it. It's between us."

Marshal let out a sigh, then relaxed back in his chair. "You're still as stubborn as when we were kids, you know that?"

She picked up her tea and lifted it toward him. "Cheers to that."

He barked a laugh and shook his head. "Ready to go back in? Mom's drilling Sophie about the festival planning. She could probably use our help."

Madison pushed back her chair and got to her feet.

"I need to talk to Sophie about that, anyway. Katie asked me to do some budgeting stuff. I've got some questions about the food budget." She blew out the candle, then looked at her dog and patted her thigh. "Come on, Mack."

Marshal followed her toward the door with Mack at his heels. "Good luck reining in Sophie's expenses. I've already promised to deliver a hundred pounds of acorn squash."

"Acorn squash? What for?"

"Who knows? Some fancy recipe, I'm sure."

Madison opened the door to let them back inside, her heart warming at the sight of her Mom and Sophie huddled over a binder at the kitchen table.

Sophie glanced up at her. "Hey, Madi, what's that program Katie told you about yesterday?"

"I'll grab my computer and show it to you." Madison strode toward the stairs that led to her bedroom, happy to focus on something other than her crazed ex-husband or over-protective family.

CHAPTER THIRTEEN

Dylan picked up a package of paper plates from the shelf in the party supply section of Lakeside Pharmacy. He held them up for his mom to see. "You think she'd like pink?"

Cathy wrinkled her nose. "She's not into pink anymore, remember? Purple and blue are her latest favourites."

"It changes every week with that kid." He put the plates back, then held out the basket for his mom to plunk a package of purple ones inside.

"You're too old to keep up with the trends now," she teased.

It was Tuesday afternoon. Dylan had taken a few hours off work to help his mom get some supplies for Natalie's birthday party on Friday.

Another perk to working at home that he would lose if he had to move—his flexible schedule. Provided he didn't have a meeting, it was easy to catch up on a few hours of work in the evening.

He grabbed a package of streamers from the top rack.

"Not those," Cathy said. "She doesn't like polka-dots anymore either. Here," she pointed, "those striped ones are cute."

Dylan exchanged the polka-dot streamers for the purple and white striped ones, shaking his head. "Who knew my niece was a six-year-old Martha Stewart?"

"She has fine tastes," Cathy said with a fond smile. "You know, I want her party with us to be special. Ryan's been gone two years now, it's important we stay close with her and Justine. We can't drift apart."

Drift apart? Dylan shifted the basket to his other arm. "Justine's always been great about keeping us in their lives."

"I know she has," Cathy replied. "For now. But if she meets somebody—"

"Whoa, Mom. Where's this coming from?"

Cathy paused, taking a deep breath. "After your father passed, his family faded out of our lives for the most part. I don't want that to happen with Justine and Natalie."

"That's not fair, Mom. What happened was so sudden, it shook everybody."

"Your aunt Cheryl and I were close once," she replied. "She hasn't contacted me since last Christmas. I've called her and left messages. Ten months, Dylan. Does your cousin stay in touch with you?"

"Do we really want to stay in touch with Andy?" Dylan asked, trying to lighten the mood. "I saw his fancy yacht and three-story house on Facebook. What a chump."

"I'm not kidding." Her lip trembled. "I overheard Justine talking to her friend on the phone this weekend. She mentioned she might try that online dating. What if she meets somebody who doesn't want her dead husband's family in the picture?"

He frowned, a knot forming in his stomach.

"I can't see Justine abandoning us. If she starts dating, I'm sure she'll choose somebody who understands how important her daughter's grandmother is."

Cathy gave him a misty-eyed look. "I hope so, dear. You know, what she and Ryan had was special. I hope she'll find that again. We all deserve that kind of relationship—not only love, but understanding and empathy too." She let out a sigh. "Your dad and I, we had that. For years. Sure, things were tough sometimes. But even when he was sick, he still looked at me like I was the only woman in the world. I've always wanted that for you kids."

Dylan stood rooted to the spot, unsure of how to comfort her. *No wonder she keeps Dad's stuff everywhere.* His chest tightened. *He was the love of her life. She can't let him go, and I don't blame her.*

He pushed down the lump in his throat. "It'll be okay, Mom. Justine and Natalie aren't going anywhere. And I'm going to figure out my stuff too."

She gave him a shaky smile. "Thanks, dear. Now," she pulled a paper from her pocket and held it up to her face, "I've got balloons on here. But I want them filled with helium, so I think we need to wait until Friday to pick them up."

"What do you have for gift ideas?"

She turned the paper over. "There's a craft kit I saw here that I'm sure she'd love. It's got all these coloured beads for making bracelets."

"Sounds perfect. Lead the way."

He followed her down the aisle. Just before they could turn the corner, Madison hurtled around it, coming right at them while staring at her phone. She nearly ran into Cathy, skidding to a halt just in time.

"Oh, hi, Mrs. Stewart. I'm sorry, I should watch where I'm going." She slid her gaze to Dylan, and her eyes widened. "Hey, Dylan."

He felt his lips curve into a silly smile but did nothing to stop them. "Hey, Madi. Imagine that, you crashing into me again."

"Ha ha." She rolled her eyes with a grin. "I'm starting to think you're the problem here, not me. Always showing up and getting in my way."

"What can I say?" Dylan shot back. "I must be attracted to chaos."

Cathy looked between them and raised a brow. "Hello, Madison. So good to see you again. It's been a while, though clearly it hasn't been for you two."

Madison's cheeks turned pink. "Oh, well—"

"We've seen each other around a bit." Dylan shifted the basket against his hip. "I told you that, Mom. Madison moved back here about a month ago."

"I hadn't realized you'd seen each other more than once."

He cocked his head and gave Madison an apologetic look. *Great. Mom's going to tell Christine about this, for sure. And probably Justine. And all the other clucking hens around this town.*

"So, what are you shopping for?" he asked, trying to shift the conversation.

Dylan had talked to her last night, but it had been cut short by a call from his boss demanding he email in some paperwork. Now, he wanted nothing more than to ask her how she was doing after she'd settled everything with the police.

He remembered her warmth against his chest as he'd hugged her on the beach, and how soft her hair had been against his lips as he murmured calming words. *Okay, maybe I want something more.* But none of it was appropriate to bring up in front of his mother.

"Poster board and sharpies," Madison replied, holding up her phone with a digital list on the screen. "I'm making signs for the dog adoption booth at the festival this weekend."

"Oh, that's lovely, dear. You're volunteering for the harvest festival too?" Cathy turned her gaze on her son. "Dylan hadn't mentioned that."

"Yes, with Pawsitive Match. Trying to find homes for some lonely dogs in time for the holidays." Madison tugged at a lock of her hair, then flipped it over her shoulder. "What are you two up to?"

"We're shopping for birthday party supplies for my granddaughter, Natalie. She's turning six on Friday." Cathy's eyes lit up. "Now that you're back in town and spending time with Dylan, why don't you join us?"

Dylan's throat went dry, a surge of panic running through him. "Oh, Mom. That's weird. She doesn't even know Natalie—"

"Nonsense! Madison would have known Justine. She was just a few grades behind you two in school." Cathy looked at Madison expectantly.

"Um—" Madison's face was as red as a ripe tomato. She looked at Dylan, as if for help.

He cringed. "Mom, I doubt Madison wants to spend her Friday night at a kid's birthday party."

Cathy shot him a familiar annoyed look. It was one she'd given him often when he was twelve years old and in his quoting-Jim-Carrey phase. "It's just pizza. It will be fun. Like old times."

Madison shrugged. "Okay. Sure. We're both helping set up at the Starlight Inn that day anyway. Maybe Dylan could give me a ride after?"

"Yeah," he replied slowly, trying to gauge if she was serious. His mom would hold her to this. "If you're sure."

"Perfect. It's set." Cathy glanced at her watch. "Well, we better grab Natalie's gift. I still want to hit Steeped in Books before Christine closes up. Looking forward to seeing you on Friday, Madison."

"Yes, you too, Mrs. Stewart. Nice to see you again."

Cathy rounded the aisle, but Dylan waited until she was out of earshot. He turned to Madison. "I'm so sorry."

She looked up at him, her lips curved in a small smile. "It's fine. It's just pizza, right?"

This girl. He fought the urge to kiss her right then and there. Instead, he rubbed the back of his neck. "Sure. We'll figure it out."

She shoved her phone in the pocket of her wool coat. "I'll call you later, okay?"

He nodded. "Yeah. Perfect. Good."

She grinned and gave him a little wave. "Have a nice time shopping with your mom."

He bit back a groan and watched her walk off. *Yup. We're taking things slow. Because my mom inviting her to a family birthday party is not a big deal at all. Right?*

The tinkling of chimes sounded above Dylan as he followed his mom into Steeped in Books. The earthy smell of incense wafted over them, coming from the tree-shaped burner on an antique stand by the door.

They followed the path through tables filled with books organized in a style he could never figure out—classics stacked with genre fiction, and big-name new releases next to indie titles. He glanced at a shelf with cover-out science-fiction titles on one end and spiritual philosophy books on the other.

How does anybody find what they're looking for in this place?

"Hello, Cathy. Dylan," Christine greeted them from behind the counter, as chipper as always. Trays of polished stone jewelry sat next to the register, and bins of loose-leaf tea lined the wall behind her. Anna stood next to her, thumbing through some papers, a pen tucked behind her ear.

"Hi, Christine." Cathy paused to examine a hardcover fantasy novel with a reptilian eye filling most of the cover. "Do you have the newest Ellery Adams book?"

Christine snapped her fingers. "Something about a murder in a pie shop?"

"That'd be the one."

"It's over by the vampire books," Christine replied. "Let me just finish up with Anna, and I'll come help you."

Dylan wandered over to the comic books next to the front counter, eyeing the colourful display. He'd never been much of a reader, but he'd worked his way through Neil Gaiman's Sandman graphic novels in college and enjoyed them.

Madison though, she's always loved to read. Her backpack had always contained the latest romcom or small-town romance novel. He swallowed, thinking back to their interaction in the pharmacy. *Girl is pursued by her awkward ex-boyfriend and has a weird run-in with him and his mother in a drug store—I bet there's no romance novel about that.*

Anna's voice met his ears, bringing his attention back to the present. "So, Raven Stone Press said they'd have the books here by January twenty-seventh, the release date. It's on a Tuesday though. Are you sure an evening signing would work best? Or should we wait until the weekend?"

"An evening signing would be magical," Christine replied. "Especially in winter when it's so dark outside. Think twinkle lights and tea—that would be a nice theme, wouldn't it? Isn't your book about faeries?"

Dylan glanced over his shoulder at them.

Anna scratched her ear. "Well, yes. It's urban fantasy, and there are faeries—but they aren't exactly nice faeries."

Christine waved her hand. "We can think about decor later. But I think an evening signing right on launch day would be wonderful. Something for people to look forward to during the week. And I'll feature the book in our book club, so you'll get lots of traffic."

Anna's an author? Dylan turned to face them. "I didn't know you were a writer, Anna. That's really impressive."

"She is! Cedar Lake's own published author." Christine put her arm around Anna's shoulder, beaming.

Anna flushed, looking uncomfortable with the attention. "Soon-to-be published. And I'm with a small press. Tiny, really. It's not a big deal."

"That seems like a pretty big deal—" Dylan's phone went off, filling the store with the siren alarm. *Jason again? What does he want now?* He shot Anna and Christine an apologetic look. "Sorry. I'll take this outside."

They nodded and went back to looking over the form, and he made his way toward the exit.

He answered the call and pushed through the door outside. "Hey, Jason. What's up?"

"Dylan! Thought I was going to hit your voicemail. You busy?"

Annoyance wound its way through Dylan's stomach. "I took a few hours off this afternoon to help my mom—"

"Right, sorry to interrupt," Jason replied, though he didn't sound very sorry. "I'm just calling to let you know we need you to come in on Friday."

Dylan made a sound of protest, but Jason cut him off. "I know, I gave you the day off. But Doug's sick with pneumonia and can't make the project meeting on Friday. We need somebody from your team there, and you're the only one left."

"Come on, man," Dylan replied, his patience waning. "I booked it off last week. I have plans."

"I can make sure you're out of here by three o'clock," Jason said. "But seriously, this isn't an option. We need somebody here. And if you want to make sure this working from home things sticks, I suggest you prove to us that it's not a hassle."

Not a hassle for them, he means. They don't care how much of a pain they are for me.

Dylan took a deep breath, pinching the bridge of his nose with his free hand. "Okay. I'll make it work. Nine o'clock?"

"You bet," Jason said, all too cheerfully. "See you then, man. Oh, and don't forget to send me those progress reports tonight."

"Will do," Dylan replied, then hung up.

Great. Just great. Now, he'd have to cancel on Marshal and the festival planning. And Madison—he'd promised to give her a ride to Natalie's birthday. He ran the math in his head. *If I actually leave at three, I should be home by five. Natalie's supper starts at six—I should be able to swing by the inn and pick up Madison, at least.*

Still, he couldn't fight the well of disappointment forming in his stomach. He'd been looking forward to his day off. Setting up a pumpkin patch and decorations for a festival would be a nice reprieve from work, and having Madison at his side would have been the icing on the cake.

He let out a sigh, then swiped open his contacts and pulled up Marshal's name. *May as well get this over with now.*

CHAPTER FOURTEEN

Madison leaned her elbow on her parents' kitchen table, frowning at the computer screen. Mack snored from his giant bed in the corner of the room, with Dolly curled up beside him. Madison and her mom had taken them for their early evening walk, then her parents had rushed out the door for a charity committee meeting in town. She was on her own tonight, and grateful for the silence while she worked. The last thing she wanted was her mother peering over her shoulder, telling her what to do.

She tapped her pen against the side of her now-empty tea mug. *These numbers don't make sense. Where did she put the money they got back from the petting zoo cancellation?*

She'd have to call Katie—who on top of everything else, also did the books for the inn—to figure this one out.

At the meeting on Saturday, Katie had taken Madison aside to ask if she'd work on the books for the festival. Sophie had told her about Madison's career as a bookkeeper, so she was a natural fit for it. But the computer program Katie used was one Madison hadn't worked with before, and she was dying to upgrade the inn's books to her usual choice. *If only this was my real job,* she mused. *Then maybe I would have a say in that.*

She logged in to her email to see if Katie had sent her any more receipts. A promotional email for dog accessories stared back at her, but other than that there was nothing new. She scrolled through the list to make sure she hadn't missed anything—nothing new from the inn, and no response yet from Mrs. Henderson at the accounting firm. Even though their only bookkeeping position had been filled, Madison had followed her father's advice and sent in her resumé a few days ago.

Patience, she reminded herself. *Something will come up. It has to.*

She picked up her empty mug and made her way to the kitchen area. She set it on the counter, then grabbed the stainless steel kettle, filled it, and set it on the stove to boil.

Maybe I should start looking at jobs in other areas. She bit the side of her cheek, mulling over her options. *Cedar Lake isn't exactly the hub of the lower mainland.* But if she moved, what would happen to her and Dylan? She shook her head. *I shouldn't be thinking about that. Not yet.* They'd seen each other for one weekend—it wasn't like they were even properly dating yet.

Or are we? She leaned her back against the counter, gazing at the sleeping dogs and thinking of her encounter with Dylan and his mom that afternoon. Yes, Cathy had invited her to the birthday party. And it did seem a bit soon, but what else was Madison going to say? It was a kind gesture, and Cathy had always been sincere and welcoming. It would be nice to catch up.

Dylan sure looked pleased when I said yes. Her stomach fluttered at the thought of his hopeful expression, his brown eyes bright with surprise. A warm tingle ran up her spine. *Dr. Theresa said to make sure I took time to think about something other than my problems with Jamie. Dylan is a great distraction.*

Her phone vibrated on the table, and her heart contracted with the memory of Jamie's heated voicemail. But it couldn't be him. Not after she talked to the police. She stared at the phone. It vibrated again, causing a sharp pinch in her stomach. *I blocked his number, and he wouldn't dare try me from another phone. Right?*

She swallowed the tension in her throat and made her way to the table. She tapped the screen, and her voice mail notification lit up. The number was one she didn't recognize.

"Nope," she said, fighting the panic in her chest. "I am not checking that. Not tonight."

She swiped her settings bar and hit the Do Not Disturb button, her therapist's words forming in her mind. *It's a good idea to step away from social media and your phone sometimes. You deserve the time away from the noise, to focus on the most important thing— you and your mental health.*

The kettle whistled from the stove, and Madison walked back to the kitchen with renewed determination in her step. *That's one practice I can put in place tonight. Me time, no distractions.*

She could finish looking at Katie's books tomorrow, after she got in contact with her about the missing return. She would leave her phone and its drama on the table, out of sight from the couch she intended to snuggle up on. *Tonight is all about tea, dog cuddles, and my new Nora Roberts novel.*

Dylan leaned his elbows on the wood-planked fence next to Marshal's shop, gazing at upturned earth before him. A layer of thin, shimmery frost lay on the soil in the early morning sun. He had promised to help Marshal pack and load boxes for his daily deliveries before his nine o'clock check-in with Jason.

Normally, Marshal was out at the shop by now, already covered in dirt and chastising Dylan for being late. But today, there was no sign of him. Dylan glanced at the farmhouse across the driveway, its robin's egg blue paint peeling from the trim. The kitchen light shone from the window.

Weird. He must still be having coffee—and he didn't even invite me in.

He rubbed his cold hands together, then strode past some empty garden boxes and across the drive to the front porch. He knocked on the door. After a few seconds of no response, he opened it with a creak and poked his head inside.

"Hey, Marsh? You actually sleep in for once?"

A rustling sound met his ears, and then Marshal's voice floated down the dimly lit hallway from the direction of the kitchen. Dylan made out the words, "Hang on, Mom", and then Marshal called out, "Dylan? Come on in. I'm just on the phone."

Dylan made his way to the kitchen. Marshal stood next to the island with his phone to his ear, wearing his Canucks ball cap and canvas work jacket as if he had been about to head out the door. A dirty plate sat next to the sink, and a black travel mug stood ready to go on the counter.

"It'll be fine, Mom. Matthew's tough, he's been in worse situations before," Marshal said.

Matthew? What's going on with him? All Dylan remembered about Marshal and Madison's younger brother was that he'd been a broody teenager.

He'd taken off to Toronto for university, then found some hot-shot editing job for a publisher there. Dylan hadn't seen him in years.

Marshal frowned and pushed back his hat with his free hand. "Okay. Dylan just got here. I have to get to work. But I'll pop over later, and we can call him together." He paused. "All right. See you tonight."

"Everything okay?" Dylan asked.

Marshal shoved his phone in his pocket and let out a sigh. "I don't know. Matthew's been avoiding Mom's calls, but I guess he talked to Dad and let it slip that he lost his job."

"Oh, man. Sorry to hear that," Dylan replied. "What happened?"

"It sounds like the company folded, but Mom doesn't know all the details yet. I should hear more tonight." He ran his hand over his freshly shaven jaw. "We just can't catch a break—this on top of everything going on with Madison."

A warm tingle wound its way through Dylan's chest. He'd tried phoning Madi last night to talk about the change in his plans for Friday, but it had gone straight to her full mailbox.

He'd sent her a text asking her to call, hoping her voicemail wasn't filled with more angry messages from Jamie, but he hadn't heard from her yet.

He shifted uneasily, unable to keep from voicing his thoughts. "Did something else happen with Madison?"

Marshal raised a brow. "Why? Do you know something I don't know?"

"I don't think so."

"Good."

Dylan's shoulders tensed. "What do you mean, good?"

Marshal snatched his travel mug from the counter with a scowl. "I dunno, you two have been spending a lot of time together. I guess it's good you don't have any secrets."

"Secrets?" Dylan followed him through the doorway into the hall, his feet thumping against the hardwood floor. "Why would we have any secrets?"

"Like a family dinner on Friday?" Marshal asked over his shoulder.

"How'd you know about that? If Madison told you, it's not a secret, is it?"

"Sophie told me," Marshal snapped back. "She thought I already knew."

How is this any of his business? Dylan clenched his jaw, marching after his friend. "My mom asked her. What was I supposed to do? Uninvite her? That'd go over well." He raised his voice. "*Oh, Madison, by the way, I don't think you should come to my niece's birthday dinner. I'm afraid your cranky brother will show up to drag you home like a caveman.*"

They reached the front porch. Marshal spun to face him, clutching his travel mug with white-knuckled fingers. "Look, Madison doesn't need any more heartache. It's too fast. And in case you've forgotten, you're probably moving to Vancouver in a few months. It'll be just like last time—"

"That's not fair." Heat swept over Dylan's face. He jabbed a finger in Marshal's direction. "This is nothing like last time. We're adults, and you know I'm working my butt off to stay in Cedar Lake."

"Are you?" Marshal asked. "Because I don't want to watch her break again. You don't know what it was like the last time you left. And," he sputtered, gesturing with the travel mug, "with the Jamie situation—"

"Stop." Dylan held up his hands, his heart sinking.

As much as he hated to admit it, Marshal had a point. What if he was forced to move away again? Sure, Vancouver wasn't that far. But the situation felt all too familiar.

Marshal glared at him, but lowered the mug. "I shouldn't be talking to you about this. Madison asked me not to."

"I mean, maybe you should listen to her," Dylan replied. "She's not the broken doll your family thinks she is. You should have seen how strong she was the other night—"

"I don't want to hear about your rendezvous at the beach." Marshal leaned against the door frame. His expression softened. "You're my best friend. She's my twin sister. You have a history. It's complicated for me, okay? It is for everybody."

Dylan shoved his hands in his pockets, trying to slow his racing pulse. "I know. It is for me too. But I'm trying my best, man. We're taking things slow. And I'm fighting to stay here, for more reasons than one."

Marshal tugged at his hat and narrowed his eyes. "I saw the way she looked at you on Saturday at the inn. This is dangerous territory. Just think about things.

Okay? Don't rush her into anything." He paused. "And figure out your work stuff. Who's going to help me and Beena in the greenhouse this winter if you leave?"

The tension eased from Dylan's shoulders, a hint of humour rolling through him. "Oh, yeah. Setting up your hydroponics system—for free—is the top reason why I'm trying to stay. Priority number one."

Marshal's lip twitched, as if he were fighting a smile. "I thought so. Now, can we go pack those variety boxes or what? Beena's going to get here and we'll have nothing done." He straightened and jerked open the door.

Dylan followed him outside into the crisp autumn air. He fell into step beside him and gave him a teasing grin. "Aren't you glad we shared our feelings? Don't you feel better?"

Marshal grunted. "Stop being weird."

"Need a hug?" Dylan cocked his head. "Yeah, we should hug."

"Don't even think about it."

Dylan chuckled, but the knot in his stomach grew harder. What Marshal had said earlier sat in the back of his mind. *What if Jason can't get the approval for me to stay in Cedar Lake?*

Things were complicated enough before with only his family to consider, but with Madison added to the mix— he swallowed, unable to finish the thought. *I'll talk to Jason and Ken on Friday and make it clear I need an answer. Even if it's a no, at least I'll have some direction.*

He swallowed, remembering Madison trembling in his arms the other night and how right it had felt that he was the one holding her, supporting her. Like his world had aligned. He bit back a groan, the weight of the situation pressing into him.

CHAPTER FIFTEEN

Madison opened the kennel door and took a step back, giving Anna room to bring Monty inside. They golden dog followed her obediently, then sat and waited while Anna knelt in front of him. She gave him a good scratch before removing his leash. *They look so good together*. The dog licked Anna's cheek and wagged his tail, making her laugh and causing her ebony ponytail to fall into her face.

"Dude." Anna chuckled and took off her glasses. "You're smudging my lenses." She got to her feet, unzipped her jacket, and began to clean her glasses on the hem of her sweater.

"It's like they zero in on the exact things you don't want them to mess up—glasses, white tee shirts," Madison gestured to the dog, who was snuffling Anna's shirt, "or loose threads on your sweater."

Anna put her glasses back on and glanced down at Monty. She guided his nose away from her shirt, then gave him another scratch. "Cute, but trouble."

"Big time. You should meet Mack. He's half Great Dane, and he leaves drool marks on the walls. I wish I were joking."

Anna laughed, then stepped out of the kennel and closed the door behind her, her hand on her chest. "I love him, though. He's got to find a home at the adoption event. People will eat him up. Don't you think?"

"I hope so." Madison was glad Anna had asked her about volunteering at the dog shelter at the festival meeting on Saturday. She was a natural with the animals. Her calm presence seemed to rub off on them.

"He deserves a good family."

Monty watched Anna through the wire, his tongue lolling to the side in a doggy smile.

Madison grinned. "You know, he seems to like you a lot. Have you ever thought about getting a dog?"

"Oh, I don't know." Anna glanced at Monty, who perked his ears in her direction. "It's one thing to volunteer here a few hours a week, but I don't know if I have time for my own pet. I'm so busy, between work and writing."

"I get that. They are a lot of work. But the drool and dog hair make up for it," Madison joked. "Hey, you said you're a writer? What do you write?"

Anna tore her gaze from the dog and dipped her chin. "Oh, nothing ground-breaking. Just urban fantasy stuff. You know—demons, druids, fae creatures. It's kind of silly, really."

"That's not silly at all," Madison replied. "You are talking to a huge fan of romance novels, including the paranormal type. I'd love to read your stuff. If you're okay with it, of course."

Anna pushed her glasses up her nose, her face flushed. "Well, I do have a book coming out, actually. *The Wicked Moon*. I'm having a book signing at Steeped in Books. You should come."

Madison's mouth fell open. "Wait, you are about to be a published author? That is amazing. Seriously, I'm in awe!" She'd had no idea that Anna, Sophie's sweet, shy kitchen assistant, had a secret life as an author.

"It's not a big deal." Anna gave her a dismissive wave, her blush deepening. "It's not like a literary masterpiece or anything. But the launch date and book signing is in January. Christine's got all these crazy ideas. It should be fun."

"I bet." Madison grinned at the thought of Christine planning a big event for the store. *She must be thrilled to have a local author in there.* She leaned her head toward Anna. "Don't let her push you into, like, reading crystal horoscopes or something weird like that."

Anna giggled. "Sophie said she'd help me keep things in check. But honestly, Christine has been nothing but supportive. And her store is so cute."

"Yeah," Madison agreed. "Christine may be quirky, but she's really the best. She used to let Sophie and I help her pick books for her orders when we were kids. I have a lot of good memories of Steeped in Books."

Her mind wandered to thoughts of her and Sophie sitting on the floor between aisles with piles of books to flip through together. Her heart twinged. Between Sophie and the inn, Pawsitive Match, and now Dylan, she didn't want to leave Cedar Lake.

She was starting her life over, and everything she longed for was right here. *I can't look for work anywhere else. Something has to come up here.*

Anna's voice broke through her thoughts. "Should we go talk to Danica now? I definitely want to sign up to volunteer on a regular basis."

Madison nodded. "Yes! Let's go." She led Anna out of the kennel area and into the lobby, toward the canary yellow front desk, where Danica's tightly-coiled black hair was visible just above the high counter. When she saw them, she waved them over. As usual, she wore scrubs—these ones with cartoon dogs all over the shirt, which made Madison smile.

Madison's phone buzzed in the pocket of her jacket, and she stopped to pull it out and glanced at the screen. *Mom? What does she want? She knows Anna picked me up to come in to Pawsitive Match.* She frowned. *I'll call her back later.* She hit the button to send the call to her voicemail.

Before they could take another step, her phone vibrated again. Annoyed, she looked at the screen. *Mom again? I should have left this thing on Do Not Disturb.*

She held up her phone for Anna to see. "I'd better take this."

"You bet. I'll get started on those forms with Danica."

Madison nodded, then stepped outside into the autumn sunshine and answered the call. "Hey, Mom. Everything okay?"

"I don't know, dear," Paula replied breathlessly. "I just got off the phone with your lawyer."

"My lawyer?" Madison's mouth went dry. Why would her lawyer call now? Their court date wasn't until January. "Is it about Jamie's voice messages?"

"She couldn't tell me. But she's been calling you since Saturday and left you several messages," her mom replied. "Have you been avoiding her calls?"

Madison's chest tightened. *Oh no.* She hadn't been avoiding her lawyer's calls, she'd been avoiding her phone all together. *Those messages I ignored—they weren't from Jamie. They were from Jane Masterson!* "No, of course not. I've just been—well, you know. With Jamie's call."

"Oh, Madi." Her mom's voice cracked. "I get it, hon. But phone your lawyer right away. She said it was urgent."

"Urgent?"

"She needs to speak with you right away," her mom repeated. "I'll text you her number, okay?"

Madison swallowed. "Um, yeah. Okay."

"Sweetie? Are you all right?"

"Yeah. I'm fine." Madison shrugged, as if to convince herself. "It's probably not a big deal. Crossing *t*'s. Dotting *i*'s. You know how lawyer stuff is."

"Call me after you talk to her. If you need me to leave work to come get you, I can."

"Oh, I've got Anna. She's giving me a ride home," Madison replied. "I better call my lawyer now, Mom."

She hung up, and a couple seconds later her phone dinged with the text message from Paula. She tapped the phone number, her heart in her throat.

"Jane L. Masterson, attorney-at-law. Kristen speaking," a chipper voice answered.

"Hi, Kristen. This is Madison Talbot, a client of Jane Masterson. She called—"

"Oh, yes. She wanted to speak with you right away. I'll pass you through to her."

After a few seconds of elevator music, her lawyer got on the line.

"Hello, Ms. Talbot?"

"Yes." Madison gripped her phone tighter. She focused on a crack in the sidewalk, trying to slow her racing heart.

"Thank you for returning my call," Jane replied. "It's been difficult to track you down."

"Sorry about that."

"It's okay, I'm just glad we got through to you." She paused. "I have some news about Jamie's trial. It's been pushed up. To Friday."

Madison's breath caught in her chest, adrenaline surging through her veins. "Excuse me? This Friday?"

"I'm sorry it's such short notice. The judge working your case had something come up, and she's going to be out of town on the original date. One of Friday's trials was dropped, so she replaced it with yours."

"What if I can't make it?" Madison's voice trembled.

"You don't really have a choice, Ms. Talbot. You're the only witness. We need your testimony, or there's no case."

Dylan furrowed his brow, trying to make sense of the report on his computer screen. The numbers weren't adding up, and the fact that he'd put this off until the last minute only added to his frustration.

The time on his computer read 4:16. *Less than forty-five minutes to get this sent off to Jason.* He leaned back in his chair and let out a groan. Next to his keyboard, his empty coffee cup taunted him. It had the outline of a power button and the words *Have you tried turning it on and off again?* emblazoned on the side. It had been an IT department gift from his company last Christmas—one his boss had found hilarious, as if they had never heard the joke a million times before.

He rubbed his chin. If he had another coffee now, he'd be up all night. *But a jolt of caffeine is just what I need to get this report finished.*

Giving in to his desire, Dylan grabbed the ceramic mug and made his way from his computer desk in the living room to the galley-style kitchen in his one-bedroom apartment.

He put his cup under the spout of the coffeemaker, then grabbed a pod from the box next to it and loaded the machine. After hitting brew, he crossed his arms to wait.

Glancing around the kitchen, he caught the bright light of his personal phone's screen blinking on. It lay on the counter next to his junk basket, plugged in to the wall to charge. *Who would call me during work hours?* He pressed his lips together, deliberating if he should answer it or not.

If it's Mom, she'll talk my ear off for half an hour, he mused. *I don't have time for that.*

The screen lit up again. *What if it's Madison returning my call?* He still hadn't heard from her, and he needed to talk to her about Friday. But that would be a long conversation. He couldn't rush it, and he couldn't annoy Jason with an extension request on the report. Not when he was hoping Jason would have his back on Friday when he asked for a decision about his work placement.

A stream of brown liquid poured from the coffeemaker into his cup, then petered out with a hiss. He grabbed the steaming cup and walked by his phone without looking at it, making a mental note to check it as soon as he finished his work.

Even if it wasn't Madison, I'll try her again tonight. We have to get Friday sorted out. His throat constricted at the thought of missing the set-up for the festival and losing out on a whole day with her.

At least when I see her Friday night, I'll know if I'm staying in Cedar Lake or not. His stomach knotted, and Christine's tarot card flashed in his mind—the Lovers. *That has to be a good sign, right? True love and all that jazz? Fate?*

He set his coffee on his desk and plunked down in his chair, then bit back a laugh. *Wow. Christine's woo-woo nonsense is even getting to me now.* But he had to admit, the thought that the card could be right was comforting.

Chapter Sixteen

*N*otice the dirt beneath your feet, the crackling of the leaves, the sunshine on your skin… Madison adjusted her ear buds, trying to focus on the tranquil words coming from the meditation app her therapist had recommended. She took a deep breath of crisp morning air, taking in the smell of pine and moss.

When Dr. Theresa first suggested meditation to help calm Madison's thoughts, Madison had told her there was no way she could possibly sit still and clear her racing thoughts. The therapist then suggested walking meditation, but Madison hadn't bothered to try it until today. After a sleepless night, her mind circling with thoughts about the trial and facing her ex-husband, she needed something to break the cycle.

At the crack of dawn, she had crawled out of bed and took Mack out to the lake trails. She had to admit, the quiet of the forest and the soft voice and music in her ear calmed her. There was something about being alone in nature with her dog, absorbed by something other than her disastrous life, that soothed her.

Mack tugged on his leash, ready to keep moving down the trail.

"Hang on, buddy." Madison swiped her phone to restart the five-minute meditation for the third time. But before she could hit play, Dylan's name popped up on her screen.

It's seven-thirty in the morning, why is he calling this early? In a rash decision after talking to her lawyer the day before, she'd called him immediately after. Part of her was grateful he hadn't answered. He'd already seen her break down once. She didn't want him to think she wasn't over Jamie—she was. She had been for over a year, even before she left. But her ex-husband still terrified her, and that in itself was humiliating.

She told Mack to sit, then tapped Dylan's name to answer. "Hi, Dylan."

"Hey, Madi. I finally got a hold of you." He sounded relieved.

"Sorry for the game of phone tag," Madison replied. "I had my phone off the other night."

"No worries," Dylan replied. "I understand why. How are you?"

"Right now, I'm wandering in the forest with Mack, pretending I'm in Middle Earth. So, not too bad."

"I'm glad Mack's with you. To protect you from the Ringwraiths."

"The what?"

"You know, the Dark Riders. At the beginning of the movie. They chase Frodo on horseback."

Madison giggled. "Are you comparing me to Frodo? I'd hoped you'd see me more as Arwen."

"Does that make me Aragorn?"

"Slay a few orcs and get back to me on that," Madison teased. "Did you call just to chat about Lord of the Rings? Or are we open to discussing Harry Potter too?"

Dylan chuckled, then cleared his throat. "I was actually calling about Friday. My boss called me, and I have to run to Vancouver for work.

I can't make it to the festival set-up. But," he paused, "I should still be back in time for Natalie's birthday dinner. I can pick you up from the inn if you'd still like to come."

Madison's stomach tightened. *Am I going to be up for dinner with Dylan's family after facing Jamie in court? Meeting his niece and Ryan's widow?*

She swallowed. "Um. There's been a change in plans for me too—"

"Oh, yeah. That's totally fine," Dylan said. "I know, it was weird how my mom invited you on the spot like that—"

"It's not that—"

"—and after talking to Marshal the other day, I realized I might be pushing you into something too fast. We can slow down, I understand. I don't want you to think you're obligated or anything."

"What?" Heat crept up Madison's neck, and she tightened her grip on the phone. "You talked to Marshal? About us? I told him to stay out of this."

"Uh," panic laced his voice, "yes, but—"

"Seriously, Dylan?" Madison clenched her jaw, trying to keep her cool. "Everybody is treating me like a kid.

No, worse than that. Like a reckless teenager who's about to drive over a cliff! I thought you were different. I thought you got it."

"Got it? I do get it—"

"No, you don't. Or you and Marshal wouldn't talk about me behind my back, making some grand plan to protect my feelings," she seethed. "I don't need you or anybody else to save me. And for the record, I thought we were going plenty slow enough. Maybe even too slow. But I guess I was wrong."

Dylan's voice lowered. "I'm sorry, Madison. I didn't mean it like that."

"While you and Marshal were discussing how to manage my life, I was making my own darn decisions. All by myself." *Okay, that's not exactly true. I was forced into accepting a court date I didn't want. But still.* Her eyes brimmed with tears that threatened to spill over. "I won't be at the festival set-up on Friday either. I'll be sitting in a courthouse in Vancouver testifying against my ex."

"What? I thought that wasn't until January."

"The date got pushed up," she snapped. "Not that it's any of your business. And it's not Marshal's either, so don't tell him. I'll do it myself."

"I wasn't going to," Dylan said softly. "I'm really sorry, Madison. Do you want to meet to talk about this? I have over an hour before my morning meeting. I can swing by the lake."

"No, it's fine," she replied, fighting the lump in her throat. "Look, I have to go. Mack's about to drag me down the path."

Before he could say another word, she hung up and shoved her phone in her pocket. Tears spilled down her cheeks, and she led Mack to the park bench that sat a few yards down the trail. He sat on his haunches in front of her, pressing against her legs. She wrapped her arms around his bulky shoulders and let him lick her cheek.

Guilt pinched her heart. *I shouldn't have hung up on him. But he shouldn't be talking to Marshal behind my back. And Marshal*—an angry sob escaped her. She grabbed her phone and set it on Do Not Disturb.

I can't talk to anybody right now. I'm sick of being treated like cracked china about to burst into a thousand pieces. And nobody gets it. They all think I'm weak.

She rested her cheek on top of Mack's sleek head, hugging him tighter. He let out a sigh and leaned into her.

And maybe they have a point. I married the wrong person, let him treat me like utter garbage, took years to finally get out. Now I live in my parents' basement and can't even find a job. Oh, and on top of that, I decided to fall for my high school ex-boyfriend who's also best friends with my brother. Yup, good job, Madison. You're really nailing this life thing.

Please, pick up. Dylan cringed as his call went straight to Madison's voicemail. He sat in his Explorer, staring at the path that led to Cedar Lake beach, where they had held each other in the moonlight less than a week ago. When he'd felt like life was finally falling into place, like he and Madison had mended their broken ties and found home in each other's arms once again.

That phone call from Jamie—he'd been afraid that would break them again. But, no. It had been his own stupid judgment. Just like last time, he'd pushed her away.

He tossed the phone in his console and rubbed his forehead, her words ringing in his ears—*for the record, I thought we were going plenty slow enough.*

He groaned and rested the back of his head on his headrest, watching the sun dip low behind the cedars.

Why did I tell her we should slow down? That's just like me, jumping to conclusions and back-peddling to save face. Why couldn't I just listen to her before jumping in, assuming she wanted to back things off?

He'd been giving her space. Heck, he'd given her a whole football field of it with that comment about slowing down, and he hadn't thought to ask what she wanted. But Madison hadn't given him a chance to explain that he never initiated that stupid conversation with Marshal to begin with. Sure, he should have shut it down as soon as Marshal brought it up. But that's what he'd been trying to do. If he could just explain to her what happened, he was sure she'd understand.

Fidgeting with the zipper on his jacket, he tried to figure out what to do. He couldn't call Marshal, his usual sounding board. That was out of the question.

His chest pinched as he thought about how Madison must be feeling right now. The new trial date thrust upon her like that, having to face the man who made her life a living nightmare. No wonder she was on edge. *If only she knew how much everybody admired her.*

What she was facing—he couldn't imagine being in that position. He hadn't even let her tell him about it before throwing another wrench at her.

And now, instead of supporting her, he'd added more pain to her situation. *I can't believe I hurt her again. Maybe Marshal's right. Maybe seeing me is the last thing she needs.*

He squeezed his eyes shut. *I had everything I'd ever wanted right at my fingertips. A home in Cedar Lake with my family and closest friends, the love of my life*—he swallowed.

After tomorrow, he had no idea where he would stand. If he didn't get it together, he could lose both his home and Madison in just one day.

CHAPTER SEVENTEEN

The smell of chamomile and lavender wafted over Madison. She took the steaming mug Sophie handed to her and placed it on the inn's dining room table. She blew over the mug, and the steam billowed across the orange-and-yellow carnation-stuffed wicker basket centrepiece.Next to them, the fireplace crackled, radiating a pleasant warmth. Sophie took the seat across from her, cradling her own cup. At eight o'clock in the evening, they had the inn's dining room to themselves.

After talking to Dylan, Madison had walked the lake loop two more times, marching out her frustration. Still without a car, she hadn't been able to go into Valley Roast for the sugar-filled latte she had craved.

But she made due with her parents' coffee and threw herself into correcting the books for the Starlight Inn, trying not to think about Dylan or the trial the next day.

Despite her efforts to numb her emotions, when she'd finally checked her phone and saw two missed calls from Dylan, everything had bubbled over, and she'd called her best friend for help. Once her parents were home from work and dinner was over, she'd borrowed her mother's car to meet with Sophie at the inn.

Now, her friend blew on her tea, concern etched on her face. "How are you doing?"

"Other than my brother betraying me and the knowledge that tomorrow I'll be recounting every second of the worst night of my life to a bunch of strangers, with the monster who caused it all insisting I'm a liar? Fine. Totally fine." Madison raked her fingers through her loose waves, panic rising inside her. "Oh, and then the guy who I was stupidly falling for—again—actually proved Marshal right. I was an idiot to think he had grown up."

Sophie set her tea on the table and leaned forward, her expression soft. "That's a lot to have on your plate, Mads. I'd be upset too." She paused. "What happened with Marshal and Dylan?"

Madison snorted. "Are you sure you want to hear about my problems with your boyfriend?"

Sophie lifted her chin. "He's also your brother, and I'm your best friend."

"True." Madison gave her a grateful look. "Remember Sunday night when I was outside with Marshal? I told him not to butt into my relationship with Dylan, but he did anyway." She picked up her spoon and tapped it on the table. "He went behind my back, knowing I didn't want him to, and told Dylan we were going too fast. You know, because us spending one day together is just too much for Marshal to handle."

Sophie tilted her head, silently urging Madison to continue.

"And to make things worse, Dylan agreed with him." Madison's chest tightened. "He said we should slow things down. We were already going at a turtle's pace. Nothing had even started yet." The memory of their soft kiss on the beach washed over her, and tears sprang to her eyes. She clenched her fingers around the handle of the spoon. "I mean, not really. And you know, he might be moving back to Vancouver in January. So, there's his way out. He can leave me here all over again and never look back."

And there it was. The truth of the matter hit her like a bucket of ice-cold water—she still hadn't truly forgiven him. *But does he deserve to be forgiven? To be trusted again? Look at Jamie, he begged me to come back every time I left. He promised he'd change, and he never did.*

"Did Dylan say that?" Sophie asked gently.

"No," Madison admitted.

"What exactly did he say?"

Madison put down the spoon, thinking back to their phone conversation that morning. "Something about slowing down and not wanting me to feel obligated to him."

"And then?"

She hesitated, taking a deep breath. "I blew up at him, he apologized, and I hung up." She winced at her words, guilt pricking her chest. "And then, I put my phone on Do Not Disturb so he couldn't call me."

Sophie reached across the table and put her hand on Madison's, her eyes misty. "I'm so sorry that happened, Madi. And I don't blame you for how you're feeling. After what you've been through, that's completely legitimate." She hesitated. "But, do you think this could be a misunderstanding? I'm not saying you should just forgive him and jump into dating him again, but don't you think you should talk to him to clear things up? See how he's really feeling?"

Madison gave her a shaky smile. "Can you please stop being so reasonable?"

Sophie squeezed her hand. "I'm no relationship expert, but Marshal and I have had our share of miscommunication. Especially at the start. It happens. And Dylan's a good man. I don't think he meant to hurt you. And Marshal—well, you know him. Even if he gets it wrong, his heart's always in the right place." She paused. "But that doesn't mean he doesn't deserve a firm talking to."

"Oh, my brother will definitely be getting a *strong* talking to," Madison replied. "He's not going to get out of this one, good intentions or not. But Dylan," she swallowed, avoiding Sophie's gaze, "he left me before. And I know, it's been a long time. But, you know," her voice lowered to a whisper, "Jamie didn't change. He got worse."

Sophie raised her brows. "Do you think Dylan is anything like Jamie?"

Madison blinked back the tears pricking her eyes. She thought of how he softened when she flinched at his touch, of when he held her patiently while she fell apart on the beach. The way he reacted with calm resolve when things went awry, like hay bales falling apart or her cutting him off in traffic.

She flicked her gaze to Sophie's face. "He's nothing like Jamie."

The clicking of heels on the hardwood floors came from the dining room's entrance. Madison glanced over her shoulder, and Katie strode into the room with her laptop clutched to her chest. Her ebony curls hung loose around her shoulders, her suit perfectly pressed, as usual.

"Hello, ladies." She joined them at the table and set down her laptop, seemingly oblivious to their serious faces. "Madison, I'm glad you're here. Anna mentioned she saw you on her way out. I was planning to call you tonight, but this worked out nicely."

Madison picked up her tea, hoping to ease her raw emotions. "Oh? Did you get the email I sent earlier?"

"I did." Katie opened the laptop and brought up the company's budget spreadsheet. She turned the computer so Sophie could see the screen.

"Look at this! Madison fixed it. All of it." She pointed at the screen. "She even scanned and organized our receipts."

Madison's cheeks grew warm. "That's just standard practice."

"And look at this balance sheet." Katie tabbed over to the next screen, filled with colourful columns and rows. "Have you ever seen financial records this easy to read?" She looked at Madison. "You completely reorganized the charts. They were a mess before."

Sophie took a sip of her tea, hiding her grin behind the cup. "She's the best, Katie. I told you."

Madison cradled her mug, unsure of what to say. "I had some free time today and might have gotten carried away." She hesitated. "You're—you're happy right? I didn't mess up the system you had going?"

Katie waved her hand. "What system? Tad and I tried our best to keep up with this but, save for a few accounting classes I took in college, my knowledge about bookkeeping is minimal. Our accountant is always horrified when we send her our books every year.

And the inn is expanding so fast. With events and weddings and hayrides, I don't have time to do this anymore, much less learn a better way."

"Seems like we could use some more help around here," Sophie said, an amused look on her face.

"That's exactly what I'm getting at." Katie jabbed her finger on the table. "Madison, what do you think about coming to work for the Starlight Inn? We're willing to match what you made at your last job. We can have a formal meeting next week about a contract and benefits."

"The office is right here at the inn," Sophie said. She set her cup on the table, beaming. "We'd see each other every day. And you could have lunch from our kitchen."

"Yes," Katie agreed. "We can discuss perks like that."

"I'll do it," Madison said, her heart lifting for the first time that day. "I'm in! I'll take it. Thank you, Katie! Er—Mrs. Hoffman."

"Katie's fine," she replied. "Well, this is perfect. I'm thrilled you want to join the Starlight Inn family."

"Me too." Emotions welled in Madison's chest, and the tears she'd been suppressing spilled over. "You don't know how much this means to me."

Katie's eyes widened in surprise. "I'm glad you're happy. But why the tears?"

Sophie got up, rounded the table, and put her arms around Madison's shoulders. Madison sniffled and grasped her forearm.

"It's a long story."

Sophie let go of her and straightened. "I'll go make some more tea. Katie, do you have time for a chat? We need to talk to you about tomorrow. Madison had an emergency come up."

"Emergency?" Katie asked. "Is everything okay?"

"It will be," Madison replied. "But I won't be able to make it here tomorrow to help with setting up for the festival."

"Oh, that's no problem. We have plenty of help." Katie gave her a worried look.

Sophie scooped up her empty cup and Madison's now-cold tea. "I'll be right back." She bustled through the French doors to the kitchen.

Katie closed the laptop and crossed her legs. "Don't worry about tomorrow. Is there anything I can do to help you?"

Madison wiped the tears from her cheeks. "Thank you, Katie." She wasn't sure she could ever express her full gratitude. Dr. Theresa's words floated into her mind. *It sounds like you have a good support system, a lot of people who care. Lean into them, dear. It's not a burden. You'll return the favour when they need it.*

Maybe it was time to stop trying to hold it all together on her own. Starting now.

"Actually, there is something."

Katie leaned forward. "Yes? Anything. You've been such a support for us at the inn. I'd love to return the favour."

Madison smiled. Now that she'd started, this wouldn't be as hard as she'd thought.

CHAPTER EIGHTEEN

The coffeemaker sputtered to a stop, and Dylan grabbed his now-full mug from the tray. He glanced around his office's break room, trying to find Jason in the crowd of coworkers milling around the pastry boxes on the table. Their first meeting of the morning had just ended. While Dylan's presence had been noted, he'd had little input. In fact, nothing they talked about pertained to his department in a meaningful way. A flicker of irritation ran through him. The entire meeting could have been handled in one email.

He spotted Jason leaning over the table, eyeing the box of muffins, and moved through the crowd of people to join him.

"Hey, Jason," he said. "Can I have a word?"

"One second," Jason replied, his thick black brows furrowed in concentration. "Raspberry lemon or plain old blueberry? What do you think?"

Dylan tapped his foot impatiently. "Blueberry."

"Raspberry lemon it is." Jason chuckled and grabbed the muffin and a napkin. "What can I do for you, Dylan?"

"Can we step into the stairwell to talk for a minute?"

Jason shrugged, then loosened his tie with his free hand. "Lead the way."

Dylan wove through the crowded room and held the door open for his boss. Once in the stairwell, he took a sip of his coffee to steady his nerves. "Did you talk to Ken and set up our meeting this afternoon about my contract? To see if I can keep working from home?"

Jason looked up from his muffin, guilt written across his face. "I haven't. Sorry, man. I know we need to get this done, but I'm taking off early today. I've got a tee time at two-thirty."

Excuse me? Dylan frowned, tightening his grip on the handle of his mug. "I thought we were going to get this settled today. I need to make plans."

"We've still got over two months to figure this out. What's the rush?"

"If I'm moving, I have to give my landlord and the renter of my place in the city notice. And you know, organize a move." *Plus, I'd like an answer for my mom. And Madison.*

Jason's phone began to ring, and he balanced the muffin in one hand while pulling his cell from his pocket with the other. "I gotta take this. We'll talk more later. Next meeting is at ten-thirty in room twelve-oh-one." He shot Dylan an apologetic look, then stepped to the side and turned his back. "Hello? Jason here."

Dylan took another drink of his coffee, fighting the agitation rising in his chest. *I'm always an afterthought to these people. What am I supposed to do now?* Maybe he'd have to go above Jason's head, straight to the source. But he hated the thought of causing tension between him and his boss.

He grabbed his phone from his pocket to check the time. He had half an hour until the next meeting. A notification of a missed call from his mom blinked on the screen.

He glanced at Jason, who was talking animatedly into his phone, then strode up a few steps to put some distance between them and called his mom.

Her chirpy voice met his ears after the second ring. "Hello, Dylan, dear. How is your morning going?"

"It's going okay, I guess. One meeting down, only five hours of listening to meaningless conversations to go."

"Long day already, huh?"

"I'll say." He swirled his mug and gathered his thoughts, not wanting to worry her. "It's not all bad. Sorry I missed your call earlier. What's up?"

"Just thinking about tonight," she said cheerfully. "What kind of pizza does Madison like? I'm going to call Buddy's and put in our order early."

Dylan's mouth went dry. He hadn't told her about his and Madison's argument or about her court date today. He tried to push down the heavy feeling in his chest, but it was no use. "I'm not sure if she's coming tonight, Mom."

"Not coming? What do you mean?" She asked, her voice tinged with disappointment. "Did something happen between you two?"

"Mom—"

"Dylan."

He bounced up another few stairs to the next landing, balancing his half-full mug in his hand. Sunshine poured through the skylight window above, bathing the area in warm light.

"We had a misunderstanding." He took a swig of his coffee, tired from his late-night tossing and turning. Coupled with the long drive into the city this morning, it made for a long day already. "I just—I ruined everything. Just like last time."

The flood gates opened. He told his mom everything, from Jamie's phone call to his argument with Madison and her court date. Well, maybe not everything. He didn't mention their kiss. Or the way Madison had looked at him that night in Marshal's kitchen, or how she laughed at his cheesy jokes on their drive back to the inn from loading bales—true belly laughs, her head thrown back as if she hadn't a care in the world. He didn't say how she fit perfectly in his arms that night on the beach, leaning into him for comfort. How when their lips met—

He squeezed his eyes shut. *Oh man, what have I done?*

"Dylan?" His mother's voice jerked him back to the moment. "Hon, I'm sorry. But you can make it up to her, I'm sure of it."

"What if I can't?" Dylan's throat thickened. "Mom, I don't want to lose her. I just found her again."

"Oh, I know, honey." Cathy let out a sigh. "She's hurting, Dylan. She's been through a lot. Trauma like that, it changes a person."

"So, what do I do?"

"That's for you and Madison to figure out." She paused. "You know, Christine texted me this morning to give you a reminder."

Dylan wrinkled his forehead. "A reminder?"

"Yes. I know you think it's hogwash, but she wanted to remind you of that card—the Lovers."

"Don't even start with that, Mom. True love and soul mates and all that baloney? If that were true, don't you think Madison and I would be living happily-ever-after? But here we are, fighting after only seeing each other for one week."

"The cards don't tell the future, Dylan," she replied. "They're for guidance. And it wasn't an omen that you and Madison would just fall back into things and that's that.

Relationships are hard and choices have to be made. And that's what this card is about—think about your choices, Dylan. Consider them carefully. Dig deep and figure out what's important to you. What you stand for."

What's important to me? My family. My life in Cedar Lake. His chest pinched. *Madison*. "I know what's important to me."

"Then fight for it. Make things right."

He mulled over her words for a few seconds. What it would mean to lose Madison and his life in Cedar Lake. The pit in his stomach grew harder.

"Thanks, Mom. I should go. I need to track down Jason's boss before the next meeting."

"Alright, dear. I hope you feel better," she replied. "Let me know what kind of pizza Madison would like once you work things out."

"She's in court today, Mom."

"I know. But you'll think of something. Bye, dear."

He hung up his phone, his lips curved in a small smile. As much as he liked to poked fun at his mother's new-age attitude, she might be right about this. Leaving Cedar Lake felt wrong. Every bone in his body told him so. He had to settle this today.

Before he could pocket his phone, it vibrated with a text. He glanced at the screen. *Madison.* His heart in his throat, he swiped to open the message.

Hi Dylan. You might not want to hear from me, and I don't blame you if you don't. But I just want to apologize for my behaviour yesterday. If your offer to talk is still on the table, I'd like to take you up on it.

He sat on the bottom stair and set his mug next to him, then texted her back with trembling fingers.

Of course it's still on the table. Let me know when it would work for you.

He held his breath as the ellipses indicating her pending response blinked on the screen. After a few seconds, her reply popped up.

I wish I could talk to you right now, but we're on our way to the provincial courthouse. My ex's trial is at eleven. Maybe this afternoon, once your meetings are out?

The trial. Guilt tugged at Dylan's heart. She must be a ball of frayed emotion. Add their stupid argument on top of everything—he had to do something to ease her mind.

I'm sorry too, and I'm so glad you got in touch. I'll call you as soon as I'm done. How are you holding up?

She replied, *As okay as I can be. Mom and Sophie are with me.*

There was a pause, then one more message flashed on.

That was a lie. I'm a nervous wreck. I wish I could have seen you before this.

Dylan glanced at the time on his screen, his mind whirling. He tapped a quick reply and rushed down the stairs to talk to Jason, his jaw set. *I can't let him push me off again. My mom and Natalie, Madison, my home*—he shook his head. *My life is more important than Jason's tee time.*

Madison stared at her phone, tears blurring her eyes. Her mom and Sophie talked softly in the front seats of the vehicle, but she couldn't make out their words. She'd opted to ride in the back of her mom's SUV, hoping for a quiet reprieve from her mother's coaching. Cars crowded on either side of them, signaling they must be nearing downtown Vancouver, inching toward the provincial courthouse.

She read Dylan's words for the umpteenth time. *I'm sorry too.* Somehow, they made everything better. A weight had lifted from her shoulders. The heavy cloud that had engulfed her since she woke up eased. *We're going to be okay. We'll work out.* Just knowing that gave her the resolve she didn't know she possessed. *What Jamie does this morning can't hurt me anymore. He and his abuse are in the past.*

Her phone vibrated again with another text from Dylan.

I admire you and your strength. So much. You've got this.

A tear trailed down her cheek, and she wiped it with the back of her hand before responding.

Am I the knight now? Because you truly are an excellent squire.

Her mother's worried voice cut through her concentration. "Are you okay back there, Madi?"

Madison glanced up and caught her eye in the rear-view mirror. "I'm fine, Mom. No need to worry."

Paula and Sophie exchanged a glance, then Paula spoke again. "Do you have your notes we made last night? And that information sheet your lawyer gave you—"

"Mom, I've got everything." Madison pointed at her leather book bag on the seat next to her, then rubbed her temple. "I can't deal with you clucking over me like an old hen right now."

"I'm only trying to help. We have to make sure you're calm and reasonable, so they can't paint you in a bad light."

"Mom." Madison sank lower into her seat, wishing it would open up and swallow her. Take her to a fantasy land like Narnia, where the evil nemesis was fictional and the hero always won.

Bringing her was a mistake. But she hadn't had much choice, her dad couldn't close his practice on such short notice. And with her car in the shop, somebody had to drive her. Luckily, Katie had given Sophie the day off. Sophie had everything prepped for the day's meals, and had left Anna and Tad a notebook filled with details and instructions. They could handle the kitchen for one day without her.

It was a gesture Madison wouldn't soon forget, and made her all the more grateful for Katie and her job offer at the inn.

Her phone buzzed with a text from Dylan.

I have no problem being your squire. It's an honour.

But I'd love to try my shot at knighthood at some point.

She smiled, for once not sure how to reply.

"I'm sorry, Madi." Her mom sighed. "I'm not trying to overwhelm you. It's just, I really want Jamie's charges to stick. He deserves jail time for what he did to you."

"Oh, Mom, I know." Madison flicked her gaze away from her phone, her self-protective walls crumbling. "And I appreciate all you've done for me. I'd be out on the street if it weren't for you and Dad." She sat up straighter. "Jane told me that Jamie probably won't get jail time, since this is his first offence and he didn't put me in the hospital or anything that bad."

Paula's face reddened. She scowled as she shoulder-checked and switched lanes, filling a gap between vehicles. "That's garbage. I can't believe how this system works."

"Part of me doesn't think it's worth going through with this," Madison said. "But Jane said it would start a paper trail, and the next time his consequences would be worse." She tried to hold onto that—her purpose for putting herself through this all instead of merely walking away. "That's why I'm doing this. For the next woman who falls for his charm. The next woman he tries to use as his punching bag."

"Doing the right thing is rarely easy," her mother replied. "I'm proud of you, Madison."

Sophie twisted in her seat and gave Madison that familiar comforting gaze. "You know, this is difficult stuff. If you're not fine, it's normal. It's okay." She grasped Paula's free hand and held it up. "That's what we're here for. For support. Right, Paula?"

For a moment, Paula looked uncomfortable. Then she glanced in the mirror, her features softer than before. "Right, Sophie. Madison, when you're on stand, if you need some strength, look at me and Sophie. Pretend you're telling us what happened."

Madison tilted her head. That had been her biggest fear in all of this, having to stand there under Jamie's harsh gaze and tell the court what he did to her that night. Facing down his lawyer who would no doubt have questions about her reputation, choices, and morals as a person. Trying to paint her as a liar.

A lump formed in her throat. "Thank you."

Sophie let go of Paula's hand. "You are the strongest woman I know, Madison Talbot. That man has put you through hell and back, and you got out. You took control of your destiny."

Madison's lips twitched. *There's the Christine in her again.*

"I'm proud of you, dear," Paula added. "I want you to know that. Your dad and I think the world of you. You're honest and good. The judge will see that."

"And they'll see right through Jamie's bullspit," Sophie said with a firm nod.

A grin crept over Madison's face. "I love you guys."

Despite the fear inside her, she could do this. She looked at her phone again and pulled up the words of support Marshal and her dad had both texted her earlier that morning.

How lucky am I? To have all these people behind me. And after this, I can truly begin to move on. I can focus on healing and building a new life for me and Mack.

She brought up Dylan's message again. *And maybe with Dylan, too?*

As her mom turned the SUV into the courthouse parking lot, Madison began to text him back.

Once this is over, I can play damsel—

"Er—Madison?" Sophie asked, her voice high. "Are you seeing this?"

"Is that Dylan Stewart?" Her mom sounded surprised.

"What?" Madison shot her gaze through the window. Sure enough, a black Explorer was parked at the back of the lot. Dylan leaned against it, handsome as ever in his wool dress jacket. He held a bouquet of orange Gerbera daisies in his hands.

Paula parked her SUV next to his, and Madison leapt from the back seat.

"Dylan! What are you doing here?" She rushed toward him, and he opened his arms to embrace her.

"What kind of squire misses the main event?"

Madison melted into his arms, a rush of emotion washing over her. She lay her cheek on his chest, then glanced up at him. "Thank you. You have no idea what this means to me."

He held her tighter and for that moment, they were all that mattered. The shattered pieces of her heart began to meld together, ready to take on the world.

CHAPTER NINETEEN

Madison took a satisfying drink of her London fog, then set the paper cup in the console of Dylan's SUV. He had just picked her up from her parents' house, with the heavenly latte in hand, for Natalie's birthday dinner.

She glanced at him from the corner of her eye, taking in the contours of his freshly shaven face. He tapped his fingers on the steering wheel in time with the upbeat music on the radio.

A new sense of hope fluttered in Madison's stomach, something she'd subconsciously held at bay until after the trial. Now that she was back with her family and friends, an exciting new job, and was facing a new beginning with Dylan, the pieces of her once-broken life finally felt whole.

The change of court date had been a blessing in disguise. With the trial behind her—and the restraining order against Jamie firmly extended—she could move on. She'd conquered her fear of facing him, and that last look at his angry scowl and liquor-reddened cheeks confirmed it. She'd done the right thing.

Dylan reached across the console and took her hand. "Are you sure you're up for a pizza party for a six-year-old? After a day like today, you must be exhausted."

Madison laced her fingers through his. "I actually feel pretty good, like a weight's been lifted. Honestly, this is better than sitting at home with my parents, listening to my mom go on about what a jerk Jamie is."

His lips twitched with a smile. "Instead, you'll have a kid climbing all over you. She's going to love you. Even more when she sees what you got her."

"What I got her?" Guilt pricked Madison's chest. With everything that had happened the last few days, she hadn't even asked Dylan what Natalie wanted, much less had the time to actually buy her anything.

He let go of her hand and hooked a thumb over his shoulder. She craned her neck to look in the back seat.

Two gifts sat side-by-side, wrapped in bright blue and purple paper.

"You didn't have to do that." She squeezed his forearm. *He always thinks of everything.* "But thank you. I'm glad I won't disappoint her."

"The newest *Rebel Girls* book will win her over, for sure," Dylan replied. "Not that you would disappoint her, anyway. She'll be thrilled to have a new buddy. Especially a girl."

Madison bit the side of her cheek. "I hope so. I know next to nothing about kids. I babysat my cousin's son once, but it was only for a couple hours and he slept the whole time."

"You'll be fine. She'll do all the talking for you," he said with an affectionate grin. "Besides, you'll learn. You'll get to see Natalie all the time." He paused. "I mean, if you want to stick around with me, that is."

Madison giggled and tapped her chin. "I think I'll keep you. And that's right. We have a few things to celebrate tonight. Natalie's birthday, my freedom, and you finally stepping into your shining armour—"

"Excuse me?" Dylan said with a laugh. They were approaching his mom's house. Cathy's screened-in front porch and hemlock hedges hadn't changed in the last decade, other than a new coat of paint on the trim. He turned into the driveway and parked in front of the garage.

"You know. Standing up to your manager this afternoon, demanding an answer—how did that go, by the way?"

Dylan had told Madison that after his impromptu visit to the courthouse, he was going to go back to work and demand Jason stick to the original meeting plan about his job situation. She'd spent the afternoon celebrating with her mom and Sophie at the Granville Island market in the city and hadn't had a chance to ask him how it went.

His expression turned serious. "About that—I have something to tell you."

Madison froze, her heart in her throat. *This doesn't sound good.* "Did they deny your meeting request?"

Dylan rubbed his chin, his brows furrowed. "No, we had the meeting. And Jason threw me under the bus. He was mad about missing his tee time.

He told Ken—right in front of me—that he didn't think the work-from-home arrangement was working. They want me back in the city full-time in January."

Madison's stomach clenched. A dozen questions reeled in her head. *So you're leaving Cedar Lake? Your mom and Natalie—and me? What does this mean for us?* She took a deep breath and resisted the urge to jump to conclusions. She glanced at him, trying to keep her voice steady. "Does this mean you're moving?"

He shook his head, a slow smile spreading over his face. "Nope. I quit."

"You *quit*?" She unbuckled her seatbelt and twisted to face him. "But what are you going to do for work? Cedar Lake isn't exactly filled with job opportunities."

"I'm going to start my own consulting business," Dylan replied. "I have some savings. And after I sell my place in Vancouver, I'll have more than enough to get going." He turned in his seat to look directly at her. "Cedar Lake is my home. My family, my friends, *you*. You were the tipping point that made me open my eyes to where my heart belongs."

Madison's throat thickened, and she reached over and stroked his shoulder. "Well, now you're more of a courtier than a squire *or* a knight." She blinked back a joyful tear. "I'm so happy you're staying."

He caught her hand in his, then leaned over the console and put his arm around her. His face close to hers, he murmured, "How happy?"

Madison met his lips and melted into his soft kiss. She pulled back, her heart thrumming inside her. "That happy."

Dylan shifted as if to kiss her again, but a knock at the window startled them both.

A woman's muffled voice sounded through the closed window. "You love birds coming inside or what?"

Dylan closed his eyes and let out a groan. Madison peeked around his shoulder. A woman with thick ebony curls gave them an amused look as she walked toward the house. She carried a tote bag with a lavender bow poking out the top, and a little girl who could only be Natalie held her hand and shot them a gap-toothed smile. They climbed the stairs and went inside.

"We're caught." Dylan gave Madison an apologetic look. "We better go inside before Mom comes out here to drag us in." He paused and raised a hopeful brow in her direction. "We can pick up where we left off later?"

"Do you really think it's appropriate to make out at a kid's pizza party?" Madison teased.

"Not in front of the family," he replied in mock horror. "But after Justine and Natalie leave, we could sneak downstairs to my old room—"

"Not a chance," she said with a laugh. "I'm trying to make a good impression with your mom." She opened the door and hopped out, then met him on the walkway leading to his mother's front door.

He took her hand and glanced down at her as they walked. "You already have, you know."

"Already have what?"

"Made a good impression with Mom. She's always loved you."

Before Madison could respond, the front door swung open, spilling light onto the walkway. Cathy stood in the doorway, her hands on her hips and a catlike smile on her face.

"The Lovers," she said. "See, the card was right."

Dylan scrubbed his face with his free hand. "Mom."

Madison tilted her head. *What on earth is she talking about*? "The card?"

"It's nothing. Christine did a tarot reading here last week."

"Ah," Madison replied, a hint of humour rolling through her. "Say no more. I understand."

Cathy stepped to the side and held the door open for them. "And she was right. She always is."

Dylan rolled his eyes and led Madison inside. Cathy gave her a warm hug and took her jacket, and Natalie called out to them from the living room.

"Uncle Dylan! It's my birthday, and we're having pizza!"

Madison's heart lifted. The leftover tension from the day flowed away. Some of the faces were new, but the setting was familiar... and so was the man who stood next to her. Dylan gently placed his hand on the small of her back, making her feel safe and comfortable beside him.

Yes. This is exactly where I should be.

Dylan stood in the entryway to his mother's porch, his arm around Madison, watching Justine wrangle Natalie into her jacket. His mom knelt next to them, helping the birthday girl pack her gifts in a tote bag. It was after eight o'clock, and they'd finished the pizza and gift opening with great success. Natalie had been thrilled with her gifts—the books, the craft kit, and a new game for her Nintendo Switch.

Cathy grabbed Natalie's knit hat from the hook beside the door, pulled it down over the child's ears, and patted the purple pompom on the top. "There. All set."

"Grandma!" Natalie giggled and pushed the edge of her hat from over her eyebrows. She twisted away from Cathy and bolted to Madison, then threw her arms around Madison's waist. "Thank you so much for the book! I can't wait to show Sarah tomorrow."

Madison's cheeks reddened, her eyes wide, then her features melted into a warm smile. She slipped her arm from around Dylan and returned the child's hug. "You're welcome! I'm glad you like it.

Are you bringing Sarah to the festival tomorrow?"

Natalie pulled back and nodded enthusiastically. "Uh-huh. Mom said we could get hot chocolate and go for a hayride!"

"You're one lucky kid, you know that?" Dylan bent over and gave her a goodbye hug.

Natalie giggled and hugged him back, then spun to rejoin her mom at the door.

"What do you say, Natalie?" Justine urged her.

"Thanks, Uncle Dylan, for the video game."

"No problem, Sprout."

She gave him a side-eyed look. "You mean *Sapling*, remember?"

He chuckled and gave her a salute. "Right. You're too big to be a sprout now."

"Alright, kiddo." Justine opened the door, then put her arm around the girl's shoulders and steered her outside. "Time to go." Holding the door with one hand, she smiled at Madison. "It was nice to meet you again. We'll stop by the adoption booth tomorrow to say hi."

Natalie tugged at the sleeve of Justine's coat. "And pet the puppies!"

"Yes, and pet the puppies." She paused. "Alright, have a great night."

Cathy closed the door behind them and watched them walk away through the window, then turned to Dylan and Madison. "What a wonderful evening."

"A very successful sixth birthday, indeed." Dylan agreed. He put his arm back around Madison's shoulder. "Ready to go?"

"I just have to use the lady's room before we head out," she replied, twisting away from him.

"Down the hall, second door on the right."

"I remember, but thanks." She squeezed his arm playfully. "I'll be right back." She stepped away from the porch, leaving Dylan alone with his mom.

He held his arm out to her. "May as well get the hugging over with."

Cathy chuckled, then walked over and gave him a squeeze. When she pulled back, her eyes were glassy with tears.

"Aww, Mom. What's wrong?"

"It's nothing," she said with a slight sniff. "Well, no. It's everything. Having us all together, with Madison too, just feels right. Doesn't it? And now that you're staying home for good…"

Dylan's chest tightened. "That's why you're crying? Because you're stuck with me now?" he teased.

Cathy shook her head, a wry smile on her face, and wiped her eyes. "Happy tears, dear. You know that. Tonight, our family felt full again with Madison here. Of course, there will always be a spot where your father and brother should be. But I don't know, it just seemed," she held up her hands, "like we were whole again. I think your dad and Ryan would both be happy to see you with her."

Dylan's throat thickened. He didn't want to go there. Not right now. Madison would be back any second. "Aw, come on, Mom."

A thump sounded from the kitchen, and he glanced over his shoulder. "Madison?"

There was no answer. Cathy pushed by him. "That sounded like something fell from the shelf."

Dylan followed her into the kitchen. Their framed family portrait lay on the oak table. The back had popped off, and several loose photos lay scattered around it. Cathy picked up the frame with shaking hands.

"Thank goodness, the glass isn't broken." She let out a sigh of relief, then set it on the table.

He strode over to the shelf above the table and ran his hand along it, trying to feel a tilt in the wood. He moved his fingers beneath it. "Do I need to replace these old brackets? Geez, Mom. You can't have this falling, it's a hazard."

"Dylan—"

"Seriously." He frowned. The brackets were solid beneath his fingers. He craned his neck to get a better look. "If that old clock comes crashing down—"

"Dylan." His mom's voice was firmer this time.

She pointed at one of the photos on the table, the only one lying face up.

Dylan let his hands drop from the shelf and picked it up. A much younger version of himself smiled back at him, lean and sharp in a suit with his arm around a pretty teen girl in a purple velvet dress. His breath caught in his throat—his and Madison's junior high graduation photo.

The temperature in the room dropped, and a cool whisper tickled the back of his neck. But it wasn't chilling. In fact, a sense of peace settled over him.

He tried to shake the feeling, then snapped his gaze to his mother. "Where did this come from?"

Tears rimmed her eyes as a wide smile swept over her face. "I keep the previous photos from that frame tucked behind the current one." She paused. "Do you feel that?"

"Feel what?" Dylan rubbed the back of his neck.

"Your father." She gestured to the photo in his hands. "I think he's happy you're with Madison too."

Dylan was about to roll his eyes, but the sensation of somebody squeezing his shoulder—just like his dad used to—grabbed his attention. *Okay, now I'm imagining things. All this ghost stuff is rubbing off on me.*

Cathy wiped a happy tear from her cheek and began to gather the old photos. "Leave that one out, dear. I'll find a new frame for it."

She looked so happy, humming softly as she righted their family photo and set it back on the shelf.

Just give her this one. What's the harm?

Madison's footsteps sounded from down the hall, and she entered the room. "Everything okay? I heard a noise."

"It's all good, dear." Cathy gave Dylan a wink. She took the photo from his hands and showed it to Madison. "Look what we found! Aren't you two adorable?"

Madison flushed, her eyes bright. "I have the same photo at home, the copy you gave me. We were so young."

Dylan watched the women giggle together over the picture, and warmth flooded through him. His mom had been correct earlier. The fractures in their family were slowly stitching back together. And while nothing could ever fill the holes left by his father and Ryan, they could move on with their happy memories and start a new chapter. One with Madison, and maybe even more.

He looked at his dad's jovial face in the family portrait. It was almost as if Dad was laughing at his ghostly prank.

Alright, Dad, he mused, *if you're still around. I'm happy you're happy. But maybe lay off playing poltergeist, okay?*

Chapter Twenty

Madison stood at the bake sale table of the harvest festival, surveying the autumn-themed treats. Packages of pumpkin and maple-flavoured cookies, cupcakes, and squares sat in perfect rows. Sophie stood behind the table, patiently waiting for Madison to make her selection.

"Wow, how late were you and Tad up making all these?" Madison peered at the decorations on one of the cupcakes—the red icing maple leaf even had orange veins on it.

Sophie shrugged. "Not too late. I have a life other than the inn, you know. Or, at least Tad does."

Madison giggled. "I'm glad he's around to keep your work-life balance in check."

Sophie pointed to a cellophane-wrapped package. "You should try the maple fudge squares. They're my new favourite."

A woman reached around Madison and grabbed the last package of sugar cookies with orange icing and jack-o-lantern faces. The treat tent was a hit, as Madison had known it would be. That morning, she'd helped Sophie create the chalkboard sign propped at the entrance, stating that all proceeds were going towards Pawsitive Match.

She shook her head. "How am I supposed to choose? These all look amazing."

Sophie gestured to the cupcakes at the edge of the table. "Those are the maple sugars I brought to Marshal's party. You were right, they're flying off the table. Only two containers left."

"One now." Madison helped herself to a container of six caramel-coloured cupcakes. "Can you box up a few of those carrot cake cookies with the cream cheese icing too? Mom will love those."

"Of course." Sophie gathered the cookies and began to box them up.

The other customer leaned toward her. "How much are the maple scones?"

"Five dollars for a package of six," Sophie replied.

As Sophie and the customer chatted, Madison wandered to the entrance, gazing at the scene outside the tent. The festival was in full swing. Couples and groups of families and friends wandered in every direction, holding paper cups of hot chocolate and giant pretzels from the snack truck Katie hired for the weekend.

The sun shone brightly, illuminating the fall foliage and bright orange pumpkins Marshal and Beena had laid out the day before. Now, they were helping kids pick the perfect jack-o-lanterns to carve for Halloween.

The booth for Pawsitive Match bustled with activity a few spots down. All morning, Madison and Danica had been introducing people to the dogs and talking about the adoption programs and volunteer opportunities. So far, over a dozen bags of dog food had been dropped off for donation. *Now if somebody would just put in an adoption application.*

Hoof beats approached, and the hay wagon rolled up outside the tent. The stable manager, Dane, sat tall in the driver's seat, manning the reins of two huge Clydesdale geldings. The gentle giants bobbed their heads as if happy to be part of the festivities.

Ethan, the stable hand Tad had mentioned at Marshal's fire, sat on the hay bale behind him, laughing amiably with some of the guests. He hopped to the ground and began to help the kids down.

Justine and Dylan sat near the back with Natalie and her friend, Sarah. Dylan jumped off the wagon, then swung the girls to the ground.

Natalie caught Madison's eye and waved enthusiastically, holding out her paper cup. "Madison! Look what I got—hot chocolate!"

"Awesome!" Madison gave her a thumbs-up.

Dylan grinned at the girl, then bopped the pompom on her hat. Justine gave Madison a friendly wave, then took the girls' hands and lead them toward the pumpkin patch.

Dylan approached Madison, his face flushed and his hair swept to the side from the autumn breeze. He wrapped his arms around her waist and kissed her cheek.

Madison giggled and patted his chest. "Hello to you, too. You're in a good mood."

"A beautiful day, a festival with my niece and friends, the girl of my dreams on my arm—not much could get me down today."

Madison sighed happily. "It is just about perfect, isn't it?"

"Just about." He paused. "Hey—is that Anna at the Pawsitive Match booth? She looking for a dog?"

Madison craned her neck to follow his gaze. Anna stood at the table talking to Danica as she filled out a form. A dog with a golden coat sat at her heels, its tail wagging.

"That's Monty!" Madison pulled away from Dylan and grabbed his hand. She glanced over her shoulder. "I'll be right back to grab those cupcakes, Soph. Please hang onto them!"

"Will do." Sophie nodded at her.

Dylan chuckled as Madison dragged him toward the adoption booth. "Is Monty a close friend of yours?"

"Very close," Madison replied. "One of my favourites at the shelter. But he's older and not many people have shown interest in him. Except Anna!"

They reached the table. At the mention of her name, Anna looked up from the form, her cheeks pink. "Hey, Madison. Dylan."

Her heart in her throat, Madison gestured to the dog. "Are you… Monty?"

A wide grin broke over Anna's face. Monty bumped his new owner's elbow with his nose, and she scratched his ears.

"Yeah. I couldn't stop thinking about him. I guess when you know, you know. Right?"

Madison's chest tightened, and she bit back a squeal. "That's amazing! I'm so happy for you. Monty, you're going to have a home for the holidays!"

Danica took the form from Anna and glanced over it. "That's right. You two seem like a perfect match. Want to pose by the sign for a picture for our adoption wall?"

Dylan put his arm around Madison's shoulder. She melted into him, watching Anna kneel beside her new dog. She blinked back happy tears, wishing she could save this moment—a precious memory she could fall back into at any time. As storybooks went, this next chapter was looking pretty great. Between Dylan, her family and friends, and her new life working at the inn, for the first time in years, her future held excitement and joy instead of anxiety and pain.

"She's right, you know," Dylan murmured in her ear.

Madison twisted to look at him. "About what?"

"When you know, you know."

She stood on her tiptoes and pressed her lips to his, the pieces of her heart right where they belonged.

If you enjoyed Madison and Dylan's journey to reclaim their love, you can read Sophie and Marshal's love story, ***Pumpkin Promises***, at:

www.jessicarenwickauthor.com

This novella is **FREE** in digital form for newsletter subscribers and has all the romance and fun that *the Starlight Inn* has to offer.

Can the man who shattered Anna's dreams help her pick up the pieces?

You can check out Anna and Matthew's story in ***Starlight Inn Book Two: Novel Dreams.***

Available at my website, Amazon, Barnes & Noble, and other book retailers.

About the Author

An avid reader and writer since she was a child, Jessica Anne Renwick loves to write cozy stories with themes about family, friendship, and of course—romance! She is also the author of the award-winning children's fantasy series, Starfell.

She is a domestic violence survivor, now living her own happily-ever-after with the man of her dreams. She always enjoys a hot cup of tea, gardening, animals, consuming an entire novel in one sitting, nerding out with video games, and real-life mountain adventures. She resides in Alberta, Canada on a cozy urban homestead with her loving partner, fluffy backyard farm dogs, four chickens, and an enchanted garden.

You can find her at www.jessicarenwickauthor.com, on Instagram @jessicarenwickauthor, Facebook, GoodReads, and BookBub.